The
Other Side

Michelle Gordon

First published in Great Britain in 2013 by The Amethyst Angel

Copyright © 2013 by Michelle Gordon

Cover graphics by Jason Mordecai copyright © 2013 Dark Horizons Media

The moral right of the author has been asserted.

ISBN: 978-1491226582

First Edition

Acknowledgements

So many people to thank! As well as the beautiful people within the heart on the next page (they each know why I love them, and how they have helped me, I really couldn't do any of this without them) I need to thank these amazing people:

Jason Mordecai of Dark Horizons Media. You are more than just the awesome graphic artist who created my covers, you are a great friend who has cheered me on and kept me going when things have been tough. You are destined for great things, and I look forward to working on more covers with you in the future! www.darkhorizonsmedia.co.uk

My firewalking buddies. This year was all about transformation, and there's nothing more transformational than walking across hot coals with people who believe in you. Big high fives to Jill Martin, Dutch, Cv Pillay, Miranda Adams, and of course Allan Kleynhans, who made it possible.

A big thank you to John and Tish Harlow, who gave me a place to stay for my Oregon adventure, which is where I wrote the very beginning of this book in April. Hugs to my CWG buddy, Molly, for your support and encouragement, and also to all the lovely people I met at the retreat. Spending five days in the company of Neale Donald Walsch was so very inspiring, and an experience I will never forget. Thank you to Will Richardson, for the incredible road trip to see the giant redwoods. It really put a lot into perspective!

Thank you to Rob Lang, for helping me to climb my first-ever mountain and for inspiring the title of this book and the idea behind the cover.

Thank you to Reuben, Liz, Mum and Elizabeth for being the first ones to read this book, and to give your feedback and ideas. I appreciate all of your help.

Thank you to my readers, for cheering me on and giving me such lovely reviews; Richard Grey, Nadina Schulte, Carole Stevens Bibisi, Helen Gordon, Debbie. And finally thank you to my fellow Earth Angels, for the work that they do in helping others to Awaken and also for their encouragement and enthusiasm for my work too: George, Sarah Jane, Magda, Niki, Shelly, Lisa, Mim and Ray.

All of those within this heart, have a special place within mine.

Mum.

Aria.

Jon Fellows.   Lu   Dad.

Liz Gordon.

Andrew.

Jasmine.

Liz Lockwood.   Hannah.

Niki + Dan.

Shelly LaPointe.   Luc.   Angie Raasch.

Nadina Schulte.

Annette Ecuyere. xxx

Thank you for believing in me. xxx

This book is dedicated to all the Indigo, Crystal and Rainbow Children who have come from their homes so far away to help the Earth Angels with their mission to take those on Earth into the Golden Age.

Prologue

In an instant, in a place where time did not exist in a way that could be understood, an Angel called Starlight came to know every possible outcome for the planet called Earth.

She was certain that without her intervention, the Universe would be forever changed.

She was also certain that it was the right moment, in the life of the Universe, for Earth to finally experience what it was really all about. For every human on Earth to know, to really understand, the true meaning of their incarnations on Earth.

She smiled as she saw what she needed to do. She would enjoy watching the events as they unfolded.

She was the Angel of Destiny, after all. This is what she did best.

Her first step was to visit Earth. Because there was a young child there who did not know it yet, but he would be the one who would initiate the Awakening.

Chapter One

"Mikey! It's dinner time! What are you doing out there?"

Mikey looked up when he heard his mother calling him and frowned. He looked back down at the tiny winged creature sat in the palm of his hand and sighed.

"I'm so sorry, I have to go now. Will you be here tomorrow?"

The Faerie nodded and smiled. "I will. I look forward to seeing you again, Mikey."

Mikey smiled back. "Good night, Faerie." He watched as the tiny being got up and with a wave of her dainty hand, flew into the rose bushes.

"Mikey! Where are you?"

With a sigh, Mikey waved at the rose bush and got up from the lawn. Brushing the bits of dirt and grass from his shorts, he picked up the forgotten wooden truck that he used as a prop, and slowly made his way back to the house. It was Thursday, which meant that dinner would be meatloaf. Again. What he wouldn't give for things to change. Routine was so dreary to him. Luckily, he had his Faerie friends to keep him company.

When he reached the back door, he pulled on the handle and stepped into the kitchen. The smell of the meatloaf hit him as he entered, and without being able to stop himself, he wrinkled his nose in disgust.

"I really wish you would come when I call you. Where

have you been? You're filthy! Go wash your hands and set the table; your father will be home at any moment." His mother continued to get the meal ready, and Mikey nodded mutely, going straight to the bathroom to wash his hands. Once he was a little cleaner, he returned to the kitchen and mechanically got the cutlery, napkins and placemats out to set the table. He set three places, one each for his mother, himself and his father. He laid his father's place carefully. His hand lingered over the placemat, wishing, as he did every night that he laid the table, that just this once, his father would actually be there to eat with them. It seemed that all his father did was work. Most days, he would arrive home so late that Mikey would already be in bed asleep. But his mother held the hope every evening that he would be home in time for dinner, and so insisted that a place be set for him at the table.

A little while later, two steaming plates of food were on the table, and Mikey was sat beside his mother, as she kept up a stream of chatter. He nodded and smiled, but his heart felt heavy. He was still thinking of his conversation with the little Faerie in the garden. He didn't dare mention the conversation to his mother. He had tried to, two years before, but she and his father had been so upset that they had done everything in their power to convince him that there was no such thing as Faeries. They said he just had an overactive imagination, and he shouldn't tell his stories as if they were real.

But no matter what they said, he knew he wasn't making it up. He knew Faeries were real. He had tried to talk to his friends at School about it, thinking that they might believe him, but they just made fun of him instead. For several months, they called him 'Faerie boy' every day.

Mikey had told the Faeries about it, and they said to him that one day, people would realise that Faeries were real. And that they lived in the same world as them, just on a different vibrational level, which meant that only some people could see them and hear them.

"Mikey? Are you listening to me?"

Mikey blinked and snapped back to the present. He put the forgotten forkful of meatloaf into his mouth and nodded.

"Okay, we'll work on it tonight then. It would be good to be able to play the whole song, wouldn't it?"

Mikey smiled and chewed the meatloaf. He did enjoy playing the piano with his mother. Despite her impatience at times, she was a very good teacher.

Later, after he had washed the dishes, and his mother had dried them and put them away, they sat side by side on the piano bench, and he copied his mother's hand movements on the keys as she taught him a classical melody that she loved to play.

They played until it was truly dark outside, then with his eyelids drooping, Mikey was ushered to his bedroom by his mother. He changed for bed and brushed his teeth.

His mother tucked him in and kissed him on the forehead. "Goodnight, Mikey. Sleep well."

Mikey nodded, his eyes were already closed. He thought briefly of the tiny Faerie again, and then he fell into a deep slumber.

*   *   *

"Hello, Mikey."

Mikey's eyes widened in shock as he looked up at the giant Angel, with massive wings studded with what looked like stars.

"Hello," he whispered back. Despite his surprise, he felt no fear. This Angel had such a beautiful and friendly smile. He trusted her immediately.

"Do you know why I am here, Mikey?"

Mikey shook his head.

"I think you do. The Faeries have been telling you about the changes that are about to happen, haven't they?"

Mikey nodded slowly. "They told me that things would be changing on Earth. That people will believe in Faeries again. They said that Faeries and Angels would be coming to Earth as humans to help with the changes, to help make people believe again, before it's too late."

The Angel smiled and nodded. "That's right. Do you remember what they said would happen on the Other Side?"

"About the Children?"

"Yes. There will be a School for them. To help them prepare to come to Earth as well."

"I remember."

"Mikey, do you think you could help them?"

Mikey frowned. "What do you mean? How could I help them? I try to tell people about the Faeries, but they don't believe me."

The Angel smiled gently. "I don't mean help the people on Earth. I mean help the Children on the Other Side."

"But how can I do that? In my dreams?"

The Angel shook her head. "No, Mikey. I'm afraid you wouldn't be able to stay here. You would have to return to the Other Side."

Mikey bit his lip. "You mean I would have to die?"

The Angel knelt down on one knee so that she was on the same level as Mikey, and she wrapped her arm around him. "Mikey, my dear, sweet Child. There is no such thing as death. You will simply be going home."

Mikey nodded, but wasn't sure. "Isn't there anyone already there who can help?"

The Angel shook her head. "No one as special as you."

Mikey took a deep breath. He looked the Angel in the eye. "Will it hurt?"

The Angel wrapped her other arm and both her wings around him and surrounded him in a beautiful white light. "No, it won't. I will make sure of it."

Mikey closed his eyes and breathed in the scent of the

Angel, which he could only describe as being heavenly, and nodded into her shoulder.

"I will do it."

The Angel pulled back a little and kissed him on the forehead. "You will know it's time when you hear a voice telling you to do something. A voice very much like mine. When you hear this voice, do exactly the opposite of what she tells you to do."

Mikey nodded. "Will it be very soon?"

"In a few days, yes. We need to start the changes on the Other Side as soon as we can."

"Will I see you again?"

The Angel smiled. "Maybe in the end."

*　　*　　*

When Mikey opened his eyes, it was still dark outside, but he was wide awake. His dream had been so vivid, so beautiful, and yet so scary at the same time. The Faeries had been telling him of their plans for some time, a couple of years, in fact. But they had never told him that he would be needed on the Other Side to help with the changes.

At the thought of leaving his mother, of dying, of not existing, his heart started to thump painfully, and his breathing became irregular and shallow. The beautiful Angel had promised it would not hurt, but what if she was wrong? And how would it happen? What about his mother? Without him, she would be so lonely.

His lip quivered and a tear fell down the side of his face, silently hitting his pillow. Suddenly a light outside his window caught his eye. He sat up and threw his covers aside, then got out of bed quietly and moved to the window. Unsure of what he would see, he pulled the curtains open and looked outside.

The sight made him catch his breath. He watched in amazement as shooting stars lit up the sky briefly with their light. His breathing slowed. He felt calm, and enveloped in love.

He smiled, and wiped away his tears. He knew then that he would be safe. Because the Angel with wings of stars had told him so. He also knew, in that moment, that he was ready to go home.

*　　*　　*

"So I won't be able to talk to you again, because I have to go and help on the Other Side."

The Faerie nodded her tiny head sadly. "I will miss you, Mikey, but I am so pleased that you are doing this for us. You will be helping not only the Faeries, but also the Angels, Mermaids, the Starpeople and the humans, of course."

Mikey smiled. "Thank you for being such a good friend. For listening to me, and for being here whenever I needed you."

"Thank you for being you, Mikey. I look forward to the new world that you will be creating for us."

Mikey sighed. "It seems like a lot of responsibility."

The Faerie giggled. "Now you sound like a Faerie."

"Nothing wrong with that!"

"Indeed."

"Mikey! Where are you?"

"I'm sorry, I-"

"You have to go. I know. It's okay. I understand." The Faerie flew up from Mikey's palm, and came closer to his face. She kissed him on the nose. "Goodbye, Mikey. I do hope we meet again one day."

Mikey's eyes widened. "Goodbye? Does that mean I am going to die very soon?"

The Faerie shook her head. "No, Mikey. It means that you will soon be going home."

                    *   *   *

The very next day, Mikey heard the voice.

"Stay inside today, Mikey."

At first he nodded and continued to play, thinking that his mother had called out to him. But after a moment, he looked up and saw that his mother was in the back garden. He frowned. The voice was too clear to have been hers.

Then the Angel's instructions came back to him. "When you hear a voice like mine, do the opposite of what it tells you to."

Mikey breathed in deeply. Just then, his mother came in through the back door.

"Mikey, could you go to the corner shop and get some milk? We haven't got enough to last until the milkman comes tomorrow."

Mikey nodded. He put his toy soldiers down, stood up, and made his way over to his mother. She got her purse out of her handbag and gave him some coins.

"That should be more than enough. You could get some sweets with the change if you want."

Mikey tried to smile, but found it too hard. Instead, he hugged his mother, catching her by surprise.

"'Bye, Mum."

She chuckled. "I'll see you in a little bit. Be careful on the road."

Mikey turned to the door, and felt as though he was being pushed back by an invisible force.

"Don't go out of the gate. Stay inside."

Mikey kept moving towards the door, even though every step was a struggle. Once outside, he glanced back at the door, took a deep breath, then headed towards the gate.

"Go back inside. Don't leave the garden. It's not safe."

Mikey swallowed. It was hard to disobey the voice. Everything inside him wanted to turn and run back inside, into the warm arms of his mother. But he remembered what the Faeries had told him, and he remembered the beautiful Angel, and the shower of shooting stars.

He reached the gate, and had difficulty opening the catch because his hands were shaking so much.

"Mikey! Could you get some bread too?"

He looked back towards the house, but didn't stop to respond to his mother's request. If he didn't go now, he would change his mind.

He finally got through the gate, and then heard the beautiful voice once more.

"Stop!"

He looked up at the sky, to where it sounded like the voice had come from, then ran out across the road, directly into the path of the green car.

*　　*　　*

"Welcome home, young Mikey."

Mikey blinked and looked around him. He was surrounded by a swirling mist, and stood in front of him was a very kind-looking old man in heavy golden robes.

He suddenly became aware of the fact that he had just left his Earthly life, willingly. And that he had come to the Other Side with a purpose. With this in mind, he was ready for the question, even though he didn't know it was coming.

"I have something very important to ask you, and I need you to consider it carefully."

Mikey nodded.

"Do you want to stay?"

Mikey nodded again. Perhaps a bit too quickly, because the old man frowned a little.

"It is not your time yet, young Mikey, you may choose to return to Earth if you wish."

"No, thank you. I don't want to go back."

"Very well. Would you like to move on to the next dimension?"

"No."

"Do you want to return to the Elemental Realm?"

Mikey suddenly became aware that he was hovering above the floor. He looked over his shoulder at his wings and realised that he was a Faerie. His memories of his life as a fire Faerie came flooding back to him, making him smile, but he shook his head.

"No, I don't want to go there either."

The old man frowned. "Well then, young Mikey, Where do you wish to go?"

"I would like to return to the Earth Angel Training Academy, please."

*　　*　　*

Starlight watched the exchange with a smile. She had kept her promise, and Mikey had made the transition between Earth and the Other Side without any pain whatsoever. She watched Mikey as he met Velvet, the Head of the Earth Angel Training Academy.

She was interested by the fact that Mikey gave nothing away of what was to come. Starlight could see that Velvet was struggling to see the meaning of why this fire Faerie had returned to the Academy to work with her.

She saw Velvet assign Mikey a new appearance, and a new name – Linen. He was to act as her assistant.

Starlight nodded. So far, everything was working out perfectly.

If everything else went according to plan, then Starlight needed to set the next phase in motion.

A visit to the Indigo World was needed.

Chapter Two

The tiny grey Faerie hovered silently among the chattering souls around him. He heard snippets of conversations, and could sense the excitement and anticipation of what it would be like to be a trainee at the Academy.

A couple of times, other Faeries had looked over to him, and attempted to draw him into their circle, but he shook his head in response. He liked his own company. He was not in a hurry to get to know everyone there, he was happy just to observe.

Also, too much external stimulus interfered with his inner vision. Back in the Elemental Realm, he had been a Seer. And though he'd yet to have a vision since arriving at the Academy, he was sure that his Sight would return, as long as he managed to find some quiet spaces. He supposed that he should learn how to exist without it, in case he was not able to See when he went to Earth. It would be an odd experience, to live without any warning of what was to come. But he would adapt. Perhaps his ability to step back and observe what was visible to the physical eye would be enough to help him to read situations and understand people. He hoped so, anyway.

When Velvet, the Head of the Academy, had assigned them all rooms, he quietly followed the noisy crowd out of the hall, and following the map that he could see in his mind's eye (having memorised the layout of the Academy from the brochure) the grey Faerie went straight to his room, number 530. Before he'd even reached the door, the purple glitter on his palm had begun to fade. Obviously it was only meant to stay as a reminder until they could remember. He entered the room and found it to be a blank canvas. He flew to one of the beds and landed lightly on the soft white covers. Before his roommates arrived, he would try to mediate, to see if he could still See in this dimension.

He had barely closed his eyes for more than a second when he could sense someone at the door. He looked up to see a Mermaid there, swimming in the air.

"Hi, I guess we must be roommates?" Her voice was quite high, and it trembled a little at the end. The grey Faerie nodded.

She swam to one of the beds, looking a little unsure of what to do. She sat on the edge of it, her hair still floating around her on an invisible current. She looked over at the Faerie again. "It's all a bit overwhelming, isn't it? I didn't really know what to expect, but it's just so different from home, I'm not sure if I like it."

With his eyes still open, the grey Faerie suddenly Saw the Mermaid, laughing and enjoying herself, with another Mermaid and an Angel. He smiled, and spoke for the first time since arriving at the Academy. "You will get used to it. I know it seems like too much right now, but you will be happy here. And you will do amazing things on Earth as a human as well."

The Mermaid smiled, tears in her eyes. "Really?" she whispered.

The grey Faerie nodded. "Absolutely." At that moment, another being arrived.

"Hello," the Old Soul said. "I'm Cerise. It's lovely to meet you." She came over to the Faerie and shook his tiny hand, then did the same with the Mermaid. She went over to the remaining bed and flopped onto it. "Goddess, I am so tired."

"Tired?" the Mermaid said. "How so?"

Cerise pulled herself into a sitting position, her robes billowing around her in soft folds. "I have not been in a body like this for many ages. My last human life was in the tenth age. I have been in the Sixth Dimension, on the guidance level, ever since. I find it quite exhausting having to be in such a dense body as this. But I will have to get used to it, human bodies are far denser and heavier."

The Mermaid was looking worried again. She flipped her fins nervously and looked at the Faerie for reassurance. He smiled back at her, hoping that it would calm her fears.

With a short beep, a note appeared on the noticeboard by the door. The grey Faerie flew over to it, and read it out loud to the others.

"I guess we'd better get going then. What does it mean about decorating our room?" As soon as Cerise asked the question, the message disappeared and another one replaced it. The Faerie read that one out too.

"That's pretty cool," the Mermaid said, looking a little happier. "I will try that later." She swam over to the grey Faerie. "Shall we go?"

Cerise slowly got up from her bed and joined the other two at the door. "Let's do it."

*   *   *

Corduroy, the Professor of Death at the Earth Angel Training Academy, watched Velvet welcome the new trainees and introduce the staff. When she introduced him, Corduroy stepped forwards and did his best to look menacing. For some reason, that was what people expected of someone who taught his subject.

Though he enjoyed it at times, he mostly endured working at the Academy so that he could be close to Velvet. They had spent hundreds of lifetimes together, but only ever as friends, acquaintances, and family. He had never been her spouse, her mate, her other half.

Absentmindedly, he followed her instructions, all the while admiring her power and strength on the stage. Many would find her intimidating, though perhaps not as intimidating as himself. Personally, he found her absolutely amazing. He loved the way that she held herself, the way that she glowed.

He loved everything about her, in fact.

Even her flaws and her weaknesses.

He went through the afternoon on autopilot, taking his group of trainees back to his class and getting them to introduce themselves, then naming the Faeries and Mermaids. Though there seemed to be some excitement about this class; to him, it seemed the same as every other class he had taught. If he really admitted his true feelings, he was bored.

The Academy held no draw for him, she was what kept him there.

He would prefer to be on Earth, perhaps fighting in an army, or teaching martial arts, or at least getting to use weapons in some way. But instead he stayed. Because he couldn't imagine not being able to see her every day.

Even if she would never see him in the same way.

* * *

The grey Faerie was both a little relieved and sad when he realised that he was not in the same group as his roommates. He was relieved because Cerise's energy seemed a little heavy, and the Mermaid was so unsure of herself. But he was sad that he would now have to speak to other beings before the day was over. Though he was not a complete recluse, he preferred to keep the company of just one or two friends, rather than meeting lots of different beings and flitting from one to the other. Knowing too many people clouded his vision. All of their outcomes and futures would blur together and give him a headache. When he was around just a couple of people, it was easier.

He followed his group to the classroom, noticing that there was a very noisy green Faerie chattering away to a blonde Angel dressed in lilac robes. He kept his distance, and did his best to tune out her incessant voice.

By the end of the session, which wasn't long, the grey Faerie had been assigned a name. Leontodon. He had decided to shorten it for convenience, to Leon. Names and labels did not interest him or bother him. But he understood that it made things simpler for the staff and the other trainees. Also, on Earth, everyone had a name. He knew that from the little he had seen while in the Elemental Realm. He had enjoyed watching children playing with the dandelions he had tended. When they blew the seeds, making wishes, they essentially did his job for him. As the Seer for his area, he had warned the other Faeries when severe weather was coming, and when the humans would be destroying their land, taking away their homes.

He flew back to his room and settled down on his bed again. He manifested himself a notebook, to make notes and draw images from his visions, then he began to meditate. Quite quickly, the pictures appeared in his mind, and it surprised him that they were of humans, on Earth. Leon allowed the visions to play out, then opened his eyes to jot down some information. He was surprised to see that at some point during those few minutes, Cerise had arrived and was sat on her bed watching him.

"Would you mind if I decorated a little? I didn't want to disturb you."

Leon smiled. "Please, go ahead. I have a name now, it's Leon."

Cerise smiled. "Nice to meet you properly, Leon." She got up and started touching her bed and the walls, whispering her requests. Soon, her part of the room looked very ethereal. Her bed was made of a translucent material, almost like glass. The covers were a paler version of her silk robes, and there were now curtains around the bed. The walls were filled with words. "What does it all say?" Leon asked.

"They are quotes, in all of the languages of this age, and all the previous ages. I love words. I love the way they are able to express feelings and images and our imagination."

Just as Leon opened his mouth to reply, the Mermaid arrived back. "I have a name!" she said, her high voice even higher. "It's Coral."

Cerise smiled. "Coral. That's a really pretty name. Did you live near the reef?"

"No, I chose it because I love singing. It's short for Coralsinger, because I was part of a choir at home." Without further explanation, she swam over to her part of the room. While singing very loudly, in a tongue neither Leon nor Cerise could understand, she started to decorate. When she had finished, it looked like a palace under the ocean, complete with flowing reeds and fish swimming around. Leon and Cerise were both beginning to get headaches. Her singing was not particularly tuneful.

They looked at one another, and simultaneously started moving towards the door. Leon took his notebook with him. Perhaps he could find a quiet spot in one of the gardens. They muttered their excuses to Coral, but she continued screeching, oblivious to their exit.

With a smile, Leon left Cerise in the hallway, and flew towards the gardens. He let go of the tuneless wailings that were taking up space in his head, and instead pictured his beautiful home in the Elemental Realm. Part of him wished he was still there, but he hadn't really had the option of staying, it had been destroyed when the humans decided to develop the land and build houses. He could have moved on to another area, but he had seen himself quite clearly coming to the Academy, even before he had been visited by the recruitment souls. He knew that he would come here and learn how to become human. He had resisted his visions at first, after all, why would he want to learn how to be a destroyer? A murderer? Because that was how some of his kin saw the humans. Soul-less monsters intent on destroying anything beautiful, natural and wonderful.

But he knew that all humans were not like that. He knew that there were some with hearts of pure gold, and he wanted to be one of them.

Leon reached the Angelic Garden, and turned left towards the Elemental Garden that he had seen on the map. When he arrived, he explored the garden with a massive smile on his face. It was not quite home, but it was very close to it. He found a tiny door in the bottom of a large brown toadstool and flew towards it. He tested the handle and found that it opened. He flew inside and saw that it was set out like a tiny Faerie house. It was perfect. He decided then, that although he would do his best to integrate with the other trainees, he would spend as much time here as he could. Especially if Coral was going to insist on singing all the time. He settled onto the tiny armchair, took a deep breath and closed his eyes, soon losing himself in deep meditation.

*   *   *

Starlight closed her eyes and within a heartbeat, she was in another galaxy, as far from Earth as it was possible to be. Before her, the Indigo World shone like a beacon in the darkness. Though the planet was Golden, the lights of the Indigos gave it a blue aura.

She closed her eyes once more and entered their world. She was used to the sharp feeling that breaking through their vibrational barrier caused in her ears. It was not the first time she had visited these incredible beings.

She stood on the golden bridge, outside the gates of the

shimmering golden castle. She looked up at the spherical castle and with her thoughts, she reached out, to connect with the shining Indigo that she knew resided within.

The gate opened in response to her greetings, and she flew through, up the path to the doorway, leaving a trail of stardust in her wake. After receiving a silent welcome, she entered the castle and waited in the entrance. An indigo blue sphere of light sped towards her, then came to a sudden stop. She bowed her head towards it, a smile on her gentle face.

The sphere transformed into a tiny Child with a huge smile.

"Angel! It is so good to see you once more!" The Child leapt into Starlight's open arms.

Starlight laughed, and her laughter bounced off of the golden walls around them, enveloping them both in the sound of pure joy.

"It is wonderful to see you again, Indigo Child. I hope you and your brothers and sisters are all well?"

The Child stepped back and nodded happily. "Yes, we are very well, Angel. What brings you all the way here to our Golden City?"

Starlight sighed. "Is there somewhere we can sit comfortably and talk?"

"Of course! I apologise for my lack of manners." The Child reached up to take Starlight's hand. "Come this way, we can sit and enjoy the view while you tell me your news."

She led Starlight to a large balcony that overlooked the city. Seeing the beauty of it made Starlight's heart soar. If anyone could bring hope and joy and light to the human world, it would be the Indigo Children.

Once settled in the golden hammock chairs opposite one another, the Child looked to Starlight to begin.

"I come with a favour to ask of you, my dear Child."

"A favour? Of what kind?"

"You know of Earth? Where humans reside?"

The Child smiled. "Of course. A few of my brothers and sisters decided to go there some time ago. They wanted to experience what it was like to grow old, to have families, to die." Her voice trailed off, and she looked out across the city. "They have been gone so long that they have lost their connection with us, and I miss them." She looked back at Starlight. "Do you bring news of them?"

Starlight shook her head. "No, though you may get to see one of them again, if you should decide to grant me the favour I am about to ask."

The Child smiled radiantly. "That would be wonderful. Ask away."

"Humans aren't doing so well on Earth, in fact, they are systematically destroying it. We have Training Academies and Schools throughout the Fifth Dimension that are training beings from other realms to become human, so that they can go to Earth to help before it is too late, but they are going to need some assistance."

"You wish for us to help them?"

"Yes, I do."

The Child nodded, her wise yet delicate face was thoughtful. She looked out over the city, which complemented her with its magnificence.

She turned back to Starlight after a moment and nodded her head. "In honour of our brothers and sisters who have gone to Earth before, we will go too. After all, what is the point of all these riches and living such a wonderful life if we cannot help others to know such wonder and beauty?"

Starlight breathed deeply. "You are so wise, young Indigo Child. I know that your wondrous energy will uplift and empower the humans." She stood and held her hand out to the Child, who took it. "Thank you."

The Child lifted Starlight's hand to her cheek and closed her eyes. "I understand that there will be challenges. I know that you have seen them. But we will do the best we are able to. We can do no more than that."

The Child hopped out of the hammock chair and walked with Starlight back to the entrance.

"I shall tell my siblings of your request and see who wishes to accompany me to Earth. I imagine that there will be many who wish to help as I do. We will be there as soon as we can."

"It is my wish for you to go to the Earth Angel Training Academy first. It is in the Fifth Dimension. You will be needed there to give hope to the Earth Angels before you go to Earth. You will be well looked after by a Faerie called Linen."

The Child nodded. "Then that is what we will do. Will we be the only ones called to help?"

Starlight shook her head. "No, I plan to visit the Crystal and Rainbow Worlds, and request their aid too. But please do not mention that when you arrive at the Academy, as they may decide not to come."

The Child nodded. "As you wish, Angel."

They reached the doorway and the Child looked up at Starlight. "Thank you, for coming to visit me again, and for asking me to do this mission. I appreciate your faith in me and my sisters and brothers. We will do our very best to assist the humans."

Starlight reached down to hug the Child. "I know you will. Best of luck, dear Indigo."

Starlight released her, then left the castle, flying down the path to the bridge. When she reached the bridge, she looked back and waved at the Child, who smiled then turned into a bright sphere of blue light.

Then she closed her eyes and returned home.

Chapter Three

Linen lay on his bed in his room, and shifted around until he could find a comfortable position. Though only reunited with his Faerie wings for a short while, he felt the loss of them acutely.

Being back at the Earth Angel Training Academy was like being back on Earth, only here he had a job. On the surface, he was just pretending to be Velvet's assistant, but underneath that, he knew that he was here to learn how to run an Academy, or rather, a School.

He thought about everything the Faeries had told him. He wasn't sure why he had kept all of it a secret, but he just didn't feel comfortable telling Velvet everything yet. It didn't feel like the right thing to do. It seemed easier to pretend that he had been told not to say anything.

He thought about his first day at the Academy. After being given a new appearance and identity, he and Velvet had greeted the new class of Earth Angel Trainees to the Academy. It was a massive class, much bigger than the one that Linen had been a part of when he had attended the Academy more than ten years before.

He had met all of the professors again. They didn't recognise him as the fire Faerie; they just accepted him as an Old Soul who had come to be Velvet's assistant. Despite his now very adult appearance, he still felt quite intimidated by them.

So much had happened that he felt like years had passed since he'd left Earth, not just a day. Linen thought of his mother, and wondered how she was coping right now. A tear slid down the side of his face, and he remembered the night when he saw all of the shooting stars. He closed his eyes and silently asked the Angel with wings of stars to send his mother a sign that he was okay, and that one day, she would be okay too.

He pulled his covers over him, and decided to try and rest.

"Good night, Mum. I love you," he whispered into the darkness.

*   *   *

Starlight heard his prayer and smiled. For all he had done, for all he was about do to for the human race and for the fate of the Universe, she felt she should do something for him in return. She closed her eyes and travelled to where his mother slept

Starlight watched her sleeping fitfully for a while. Her face was creased in anguish, her eyes were puffy and a handkerchief was clutched in one hand. Her husband was lying on the other side of the bed, as distant and cold in sleep as he ever was when awake.

Starlight closed her eyes again and entered both of their dreams. With her thoughts, she brought them both into the same dreamspace dimension.

"What are you doing here?" Mikey's mother asked her husband. She looked around the space, which was a beautiful garden.

He shrugged. "I don't know. Where are we?"

She shook her head. "I don't know. But I wonder-"

"Mum! Dad!"

They both looked up and saw Mikey running towards

them.

His mother fell to her knees and held her arms out. Mikey ran into them and she held him close, crying and laughing at the same time.

"Mikey! Are you okay?"

Mikey pulled back and nodded, a smile on his face. "Of course I am! I'm in such a beautiful place, Mum, you would love it here."

His mum smiled. "I thought I had lost you forever."

"You can never lose me, Mum, I will always be with you." Mikey looked up at his dad, who was still stood awkwardly to the side. "I'll always be with you too, Dad."

His father nodded, and tears began to run down his face. Mikey held his hand out to him, and his father stepped forwards to take it. He wrapped his arms around both his son and wife and held them tight.

"I love you, Mum, I love you, Dad."

His parents murmured the same words in response.

Mikey pulled away, "I have to go now." He put their hands in each other's. "But you will be okay, I just know it. And I will see you again. If you miss me though, you can always go and talk to the Faeries at the bottom of the garden, they will keep you company."

For the first time, they did not laugh, nor ridicule his comments about the Faeries. They just nodded.

Mikey walked a few steps, then turned back to wave. "'Bye, Mum. 'Bye, Dad."

*　　　*　　　*

When Starlight opened her eyes, Mikey's mother and father were wrapped in each other's arms, and his mother's face had smoothed out and relaxed. Starlight smiled. She felt that Linen's prayer had been answered, and that they would be okay now.

She closed her eyes again and returned home once more.

*   *   *

When Linen opened his eyes the next day, he felt a sense of peace wash over him. He knew that he was in the right place, doing the right thing. He got up and stretched, then prepared himself for the coming day.

But he couldn't have predicted what was going to happen. It seemed that Velvet had really liked the tune he was humming the day before, so she had manifested a piano for him to play it for her. His mother had never finished teaching it to him, so it would be an interesting challenge.

He was sat at the piano, wondering how this fit into his mission to learn how to run the Academy. He couldn't help but feel that Velvet had just been glad not have him around for the rest of the day. He played a few notes and smiled. He didn't really mind this assignment though. It reminded him of his mother. Somehow, he just knew that she was okay. That she would cope without him.

He lost himself in the music, resolving to go with the flow more, and not worry too much if he was headed in the right direction. Because surely the Angel of the stars would visit him again to tell him if he was heading off course?

*   *   *

Having spent the rest of the evening in the little Faerie house, only slipping back into his bed after Cerise and Coral were asleep, Leon had missed the arrival of the Starpeople from Zubenelgenubi. The first he knew of it was when he passed a glowing being on his way to his first class the next morning. He had not Seen their arrival, but then his focus had been elsewhere.

He arrived at Death 666, where his classmates stood

waiting in line outside.

"I think he looked very scary on the stage yesterday," said the tiny chattering green Faerie, who had been named Aria the previous day.

Amethyst, her Angel friend, nodded back.

"Is that because death is scary?"

"I think it's because humans find the concept of death to be a scary one, and Professor Corduroy is teaching us what humans believe," Amethyst said.

"I get it. But still, you don't think he'll do anything scary today do you? I mean, it's only the first day," Aria's words died as the door disappeared. There was no one stood here to greet them, instead, the room was darkened and creepy music filtered out into the hallway. As he followed his classmates into the room, Leon straightened his shoulders and tried to be strong for what he knew would not be an easy lesson.

*   *   *

Corduroy was having so much fun. He always did something dramatic for his first class, and there was nothing quite as dramatic as wearing a long black coat and wielding a machine gun.

Velvet wouldn't be visiting until his second class, so he could do something tamer then. She didn't agree with his methods, she thought that he should teach the trainees about death in a softer, kinder way. But death wasn't particularly soft or kind, unless you happened to die quietly in your sleep. Mostly, death was ugly and painful and shocking, and that was what he tried to get across to them, so that they wouldn't be so shocked when they got to Earth. He surveyed the classroom and nodded in satisfaction. He had hidden himself, started the creepy music, and then allowed the door to open to his trainees. They had all filed in cautiously, sticking together, moving as a solid group. Well, that wouldn't do. He set about dividing them up by throwing a grenade in their midst. They all leapt away in separate directions, and then when it exploded, the screaming began.

Of course, in this dimension, it was all just smoke and noise. There was no actual danger.

But they didn't know that.

He had fake people standing around, who he shot at, 'killing' them. He started laughing manically, and he snuck a peek at his terrified trainees scattered about. The Angels didn't seem to be scared, just sad. He guessed they had already seen terror like this before.

He was just getting into the role when suddenly everything disappeared, the music stopped and the room lightened up.

He turned to the door and saw her standing there. His heart began to speed up a little and he smiled at her.

"Ah ha! Hello, Velvet! Welcome to Death 666."

*   *   *

The Indigo Child left her castle, and moved at the speed of light to the meeting circle. She hovered in the centre and sent her light out in twelve spokes. Her brothers and sisters responded to her silent call and moved quickly from all areas of the Golden City, taking their places along the spokes of light. They then connected to one another with threads of light between them, forming an Indigo blue spider web.

Silently, the web hovered in the meeting circle as she told them about her visit from the Angel.

"Brothers and sisters, I have brought you all here now to discuss a matter of great importance. I was visited by the Angel of the stars a little earlier, and she has asked me if we would go to Earth."

There was a murmuring throughout the web, and with a thought, she silenced them.

"Our light and love is needed on Earth to help with the Spiritual Awakening, without us, it may not happen. I know that it worries you, that we may lose our connection with one another, but I know we can find a way to keep the connection alive."

She paused, to see if there were any comments. There were none.

"I will not force anyone to come with me, it will be entirely your decision. Should you choose to come with me, we will be leaving as soon as we are able. We will be going to the Fifth Dimension first, and then our souls will be called to Earth from there. Please, think about it carefully. I understand that you may not want to leave our Golden City. I, too, will be sad to leave, but I know that it is for the good of the Universe. If you wish to come with me, please come here when the second star has passed the Purple Planet. Thank you for your attendance and attention."

She silently dismissed her siblings and pulled her light back in again, breaking thought contact. She moved back to the castle, to prepare for their coming mission.

*   *   *

It was his favourite garden. And tonight, he had it all to himself. It seemed that the first day of classes must have taken its toll on the trainees, because the Atlantis Garden was empty and quiet when he reappeared next to the bench. He wasn't sure why he liked to sit on this particular bench, especially considering it had the best view of his arch enemy.

Corduroy sighed. Arch enemy was probably a bit dramatic. He stared at the golden statue, with its perfect, gleaming body and piercing emerald eyes.

He wasn't sure why he had created it. He thought that part of the reason was that it made him feel better. Because he was in Velvet's life, and Laguz wasn't. Laguz was just a hazy memory. So why hadn't Velvet moved on? Why didn't she realise that she loved Corduroy? He had been there for her, in every lifetime, though at times he felt that she hadn't realised it was him. In so many of those lifetimes it would have been possible for them to be together, but she had never fallen for him.

He had also created the statue as a gift for Velvet, to give her something as a reminder of her life with Laguz in Atlantis. Despite appearing quite selfish at times, he genuinely wanted her to be happy. Not that she'd ever thanked him for it, of course.

Corduroy sighed. He had a feeling that everything was about to change. He wondered, yet again, whether she would have decided to be with him if he had just admitted how he felt about her. It was purely his pride that kept him waiting, and hoping, that she would realise it by herself.

Corduroy wished he hadn't waited so long. He resolved to tell her, soon.

*   *   *

Leon decided to spend the evening in his room at the end of the long day, knowing that once he had relaxed, he would not want to move. Before returning to the room, he had gone for a wander and had seen Coral in the Underwater Garden, laughing and joking with a couple of other Mermaids, and also an Angel. It was the exact same scene as the vision he had experienced the day before. Which confirmed to him that his Sight was indeed still intact.

He arrived back at the room and found Cerise lying on her bed, her eyes closed. Leon flew in quietly and softly landed on his own bed. His side of the room had remained plain white, and he considered decorating it, as his roommates had, but he actually liked the plainness of it. It contrasted nicely with all of the images in his mind. He didn't need any external imagery, it was all within.

He crossed his tiny legs and his wings closed. He took in

a deep breath and let his eyes drift shut. Almost immediately, he had a clear image of a golden city, so beautiful it didn't look like it could possibly be real. There were no people though, it was empty. This made him feel a little sad, but at the same time, the image gave him an incredible sense of hope that lifted him up. He could feel the heaviness and gloom of his earlier Death class completely falling away, and Leon knew, then, that everything would work out.

"Are you asleep?"

Leon opened his eyes and the golden city faded away. Cerise was sat up on her bed, looking at him. He shook his head. "Even Faeries don't sleep sitting up."

Cerise chuckled. "I'm sorry, I haven't spent much time with Faeries. Are you really an Oracle?"

"I am a Seer, yes."

"So you See the future?"

"Sometimes, if I am supposed to. A lot of the time, I See things that are happening in the current moment. But in another dimension, realm or planet."

"What is the purpose of your visions? Why do you think you have them?"

Leon shrugged. "In the Elemental Realm, they were quite useful, I could predict the weather and I could warn the Elementals when there was danger nearby. But here," he shook his head. "Since I arrived, I have had many that haven't made much sense to me." He reached into his tiny pocket and pulled out his notebook and pencil. "Which is why I've been writing them down, just in case they have any significance and I need to remember them later." He flicked to a clean page and did a quick sketch of the golden city, before it completely faded from his mind.

Cerise was respectfully quiet while he sketched. When he had finished, he tucked the notebook away and looked up at her. "I asked Velvet earlier, why there were Old Souls at the Academy, seeing as they have been human before, and she said it may have been a while since they had been to Earth, so the training here was a reminder to them of what it is like."

"It's true, this age is very different to the ones I lived in. And as I said yesterday, it takes time to get used to the heavy bodies again. Also, we need to connect with other Earth Angels before we go to Earth, to increase our chances of Awakening. It's all about preparation. Without this time here, most of us are more likely to exit early, because we know that ultimately, we do not need to be on Earth for our own purposes of evolution. We are there to help with the Awakening, to help other Earth Angels and humans. We are not there for ourselves."

Leon nodded. "It was good of you to come then."

Cerise shrugged. "When we were asked to volunteer, it seemed like a good idea. After all, there is no point in staying on the guidance level and leaving the Earth to be destroyed by humankind. Without Earth, who will we guide?"

Leon smiled. "If it helps at all, I have a feeling that we will succeed in our missions on Earth."

"Have you Seen it?" Cerise asked, looking a little less weary suddenly.

Though he had not literally Seen their success, the feeling of hope and wonder he'd had when he Saw the golden city was all the proof he needed.

"Yes, yes I have."

Chapter Four

Starlight watched the progress of the Indigo Children's journey and was happy to see that so many of them had volunteered to help on Earth. They were such beautiful souls, she knew that their presence would help with the Awakening enormously. But there was no time to rest (indeed because there was no such thing as time) and so Starlight needed to put the next phase of her plan into motion. She closed her eyes and opened them when she hovered before the sparkling Crystal World. The brightness of it was nearly as blinding as the fireball the humans called the sun.

She closed her eyes and entered their world. She silently arrived in a field of the most glorious lilacs and lilies. She flew forwards, to the mouth of the cave at the edge of the field. Though it was dark inside, when she went in, her eyes adjusted immediately. Her wings lit up the space around her, and sparkles of white shone back at her from every wall. She walked towards a large crystal point.

Then she began to sing. Her Angelic voice filled the cave, lighting it up with her melody of love and wonder.

A moment later, the quartz crystal point in front of her transformed into the most beautiful Child, with long blonde hair and piercing eyes.

Her face broke into a beautiful smile when she saw Starlight.

"Angel! You have such a beautiful voice. What a wonderful way to awaken. What brings you here to our world?"

"I have come to ask the Crystal Children for their help. I wish to help the planet Earth to experience the Golden Age, for the very first time. And to do so, I need the help of the Children."

The Child's eyes widened. "Do you think it is possible? We have been sending Crystals to Earth for many years now, and in our true forms we have witnessed the Earth declining rapidly. I thought that perhaps it was too late for them to experience what we have here?"

Starlight sighed. "I know they have made a mess of things, and I know that you have tried, with your energy, to bring love and hope and healing to the planet. But I feel that now it is time for the Crystal Children to go to Earth, as humans."

"As humans? You wish for us to be born on Earth and live human lives? Not as Crystals of the Earth? That is an interesting idea. It has never been done before."

"I know, which is why I think it will work this time. There are a large number of Indigo Children, Angels, Faeries, Mermaids and Starpeople being trained at this very moment to do the same. I will also be seeking help from the other Children of the Universe."

The Child was quiet for a moment. "If beings from the other realms, dimensions and galaxies are all going to Earth to help, then I cannot see how we can stay here and not do what we can to help also. I just fear that my fellow Crystals and I will not fit into the fast pace that Earth now has. We are slow, gentle beings. We will not fit in easily."

"I believe that the Earth Angels and Indigos will be able to change the world enough, so that when you arrive there, you will be understood, and you will not be forced to conform."

"I will have to consult with my family. I'll go, but I will not make anyone go who does not wish to."

"Of course, I only ask for those who are willing to go."

"When must we leave?"

"As soon as you are able to. The Indigos are already making their way through the Universe. I have asked them to go to the Fifth Dimension, to the Earth Angel Training Academy. You will meet them there. They know what needs to be done. I will send a message to Linen, when you arrive. He is going to be running the School for the Children of the Golden Age."

"The Golden Age," the Child repeated. "It will not be an easy journey or task. I assume there is a chance it may not happen at all, that our efforts may not work?"

Starlight sighed, and looked down at the glittering cave floor. "My dear Crystal Child, I cannot lie to you, there is always a chance that things will not work the way I plan them to. But I promise you that I am doing the best I can to make everything go smoothly. Even then, you are right, it will not be an easy task."

The Child nodded. Then she straightened her shoulders and smiled, her beautiful face shining brightly. "We will do our best to make it happen. We shall not let the Angels down."

Starlight smiled back. "I have every faith in you. Thank you, I appreciate all that you will do. Make sure when you arrive at the Academy, that Linen knows that your classes must commence immediately. The Indigos will start being called before the Earth Angel Trainees have all left. Time will move very quickly, and it is important that you have time to work with the Indigos and with Linen and his staff before you too, are called."

"Thank you, Angel. I will remember everything you have told me. And I will remain open to your communications should you have any further instructions."

Starlight bowed her head to the Crystal Child, and without another word, left the cave. Outside, in the sunlit field of lilacs and lilies, she breathed the scent in deeply, taking it with her, to her home in the stars.

*   *   *

"Are you sure we should do this?" Mica asked Emerald. She looked up at him and smiled.

"I thought we had already decided? To go back to the Academy to be taught by Velvet and then return to Earth?"

"Yes, I know we had decided that, but what if we lose each other? What if we are split up? We didn't even meet in any of our previous lifetimes. What if we don't find each other in the next one?"

Emerald sighed and stepped into his embrace. "It is a risk, you're right. But things are changing rapidly on Earth, and I really think that we can make a difference. Also, I believe that we need to ensure that the Earth Angels returning at this time know about the reunion of the Flames. It will give them hope."

"Do you think so? Won't it just make them think that the world is ending?"

"It may well be ending, we do not know for certain. But at least if we can reunite some Flames they would get to experience the bliss of being with their Twin before the end."

Mica smiled and pulled back a little from Emerald. "As always, you know what to say to quell my fears." He leaned down and kissed her gently, wondering if being on Earth with her could possibly be any better than being with her in the Angelic Realm. "If we leave now, we should arrive with the others."

Emerald grinned and kissed him back. "Let's go."

*   *   *

Leon was curled up in the squishy armchair in the toadstool house when the vision came to him suddenly, making him jump a little. Scores of souls, all with a human appearance on the outside, but with inner cores from other realms, walked past him, on their way to the Academy. He tried to count them but quickly gave up.

Why were they coming to the Academy? He could sense that they'd all had recent lives on Earth, that they were not trainee Earth Angels. The images faded from Leon's inner eye and he jotted down a few notes. His tiny notebook was filling up quickly, as his visions seemed to be coming more regularly. Leon had also been getting visions of himself on Earth, travelling around in a bus-like vehicle. These visions were more blurry and indistinct though, and Leon got the feeling that they were subject to change depending on the decisions and choices made by himself and the other Earth Angels that he would encounter.

Leon closed his notebook and put it back in his pocket. He had hoped that by now he would have Seen some visions of how the Awakening would come about, his role in it, and whether the human race would survive and move into the new age. But mostly he just Saw more immediate occurrences.

He had Seen that sometime before he was called to Earth, Velvet would be coming to him for help. At first, he had dismissed the notion as ridiculous, but after having the same vision three times, he decided that perhaps there was some truth in it. He would just have to wait; it was clear that Velvet would have to be the one to approach him.

He looked at the tiny clock he had manifested for the little toadstool house, and sighed. He would need to get going if he was going to make it to his next class on time. He certainly didn't want to make the already moody Professor of Human Culture any more miserable.

*   *   *

Corduroy didn't mind the extra work, after all, it broke up the tediousness of his classes, but he wished that it had been

Velvet who had asked him to do it, not her assistant, Linen.

He growled a little to himself when he thought of Linen. What was so special about him that Velvet had chosen him to be her assistant? Corduroy would have given anything to work with Velvet in such close quarters every day, and he knew that Tartan had been after a higher position ever since he had joined the Academy.

But instead, some bumbling red-haired, orange-eyed freak got the job? It made no sense.

He had arranged for all of the new students to meet him in a large room away from the rest of the trainees. For some unknown reason, the Academy was now taking on former Earth Angels, re-training them and sending them back to Earth. They already had their human appearances, so Linen had instructed him to keep them away from the other trainees if possible.

Corduroy liked the feeling of power when stood in front of the large group. He opened his arms like Velvet usually did.

"Welcome! My name is Corduroy, and I am a professor here at the Academy. Velvet was otherwise engaged this evening, and has asked me to welcome you, guide you to your rooms and answer any questions you may have. My knowledge of your schedule here at the Academy is non-existent, but I can, however, answer general questions."

He looked around the group and smiled, trying to look welcoming rather than menacing, for once.

"Any questions?"

Hands shot up across the room and he sighed. It was going to be a long night.

*   *   *

"Professor Corduroy certainly has no idea what's happening right now. Do you think that Velvet does either?"

Emerald looked up at Mica and shook her head. "I don't

know. I hope so. I know this is all very new and untried. I mean, scores of Earth Angels returning to Earth not long after their last incarnations? It could cause havoc. And how will things be different this time? How will we not just end up leaving again?"

Mica watched the waterfall silently for a while, and Emerald fell silent too. He loved the Angelic Garden. They had found it after their rather disappointing session with the Professor of Death. They hadn't even bothered exploring the other gardens, this one suited them perfectly. There was a golden bench directly in front of the waterfall that looked like falling diamonds in the ever-present sun. It reminded him of being in their home in the Angelic Realm. His grip tightened on Emerald's hand and a sense of foreboding fell on him. He still wished that they could have stayed in their home. He really didn't want to lose Emerald again, and somehow, he had the feeling that there was no way he could avoid that inevitability.

"What are you thinking, my love?" Emerald whispered.

Mica sighed. She was so sensitive and so connected to him, she could instantly sense the shift in his mood. He knew he shouldn't lie, but he hated to keep stating his fears. "I was thinking that I love you." He turned to her, and his energy lifted at the sight of her beautiful smile. "I love you more than I can even begin to express. And I know that we will find a way to be together, and we will find a way to reunite the Flames. Because I know that this is what we are meant to do." The words flowed from his lips with little thought behind them, and Mica felt their truth resonate with him deeply. He knew from Emerald's expression that it resonated with her too.

"I love you. And you are right of course. We will find a way, and if there isn't one, we will make a way."

Mica smiled at her determination. "Of course we will. But for now, I think that we just enjoy this moment."

Emerald nodded and rested her head on his shoulder. Mica

rested his cheek against her hair and knew that though he would be tested in the days to come, he would not let his Flame down.

*   *   *

Starlight heard Magenta's whispered prayer after her conversation with Gold and she smiled a little. A Seer who could not See which path to take. It was almost funny. But Starlight knew that it really was no laughing matter. She kind of envied Magenta in a way. Being able to See all that was about to transpire was not the best way to exist. Starlight decided to give her a few extra visions though, just to help nudge her along. She needed Magenta on Earth for the Awakening to happen.

Starlight saw Gold return to his usual post, just outside of the Angelic Realm, and watched him while he sat deep in thought, a slight frown on his weathered face. He sighed deeply and though he could not hear her, she sighed in response. Though he was a deeply wise Elder, Starlight knew that there were many things he did not know. She wished she could lessen his burdens, and make him feel better, but they had decided long ago that this was how things were to be. At some point soon, she knew that they would talk, and he would ask. He would want to know what the future held for Earth and her inhabitants. She knew it was best he didn't know, that he continued his mission unaware of the bigger picture. But she also knew that she would have no choice but to show him.

Starlight checked on everyone else, watching their actions as though she were observing a chess game in play. Each piece was moving seemingly of their own accord, but in reality, they were being moved by the higher vibration that surrounded them. If one of the pieces should be taken too soon, then the whole future that Starlight had foreseen would disappear.

                    *   *   *

Linen returned to his room, feeling worried about Velvet. He had played her the song on the piano, and when he had finished and looked up, her eyes were closed but tears were streaming down her face. Remembering her previous reaction to his concern for her, he had approached her quietly and asked her if she was okay. She seemed to be surprised by her wet face, and tried to hide it when she asked him to leave. He hadn't wanted to, but he had great respect for Velvet, and if she didn't want him there, then it was best he left.

He sat on his bed, and stared at the wall for a while. His foot started tapping on the floor and the noise seemed to echo around the room. The wall was covered in his notes for the School, but he had made sure that he was the only one who could see them. His mind was racing a million miles an hour, as he tried to process everything that was happening and everything he was planning. Finally, he couldn't look at the words any longer. Though he felt he should stay for a while in case Velvet needed him, he realised that she could find him wherever he happened to be, so whether he was in his room or not, it really didn't make much difference. With that thought in mind, he got up and set off for the gardens.

He loved the gardens, they were breath-taking. His favourite was the Elemental Garden, of course. He felt so at home there. In the odd moment when he hadn't been busy with Velvet, he would spend time there, among the giant flowers and the brightly coloured toadstools.

He climbed up on one, hidden from the path in case anyone should spot him and wonder why he was there. A moment later, he spotted a grey Faerie leaving from a tiny door in the side of the toadstool next to him. He stayed still, and though the Faerie looked all around before flying away, he didn't see Linen sat up on top. Linen didn't recognise the Faerie, but then there were so many of them fluttering around the Academy, it was difficult to keep track.

As Linen watched him fly away, he wondered why the Faerie had taken to hiding in the Elemental Garden. He laughed softly to himself then, when it dawned on him that he was doing the exact same thing. Perhaps hiding every once in a while was not a bad thing. Everyone needed a bit of time and space to themselves.

With that thought, it was as though Linen had given himself permission to relax, and the tension drained from his shoulders. He lay back on the top of the toadstool, and watched the fluffy clouds float across the blue sky. That was one thing he loved about being in the Fifth Dimension - it never rained. He let go of all his stress of trying to learn how to run the Academy, all of his worry about Velvet, and even the lingering longing for his Earth mother.

He breathed in the scent of the roses nearby, inhaling deeply and slowly. Everything would work out, he was sure of it.

*   *   *

After his meeting with Velvet in the Atlantis Garden, Corduroy couldn't bear to look at Laguz any longer. He clicked his fingers and reappeared in his darkened office.

She had forgotten about her Flame. Her memories of Laguz had been erased. And to think, all this time, Corduroy had assumed that she never spoke of him because it hurt too much. If he'd realised she didn't remember him, Corduroy would have removed the statue and declared his true feelings for her.

Instead, he had just told her everything. That she and Laguz were Twin Flames. That their last lifetime together had been in Atlantis, and that she saved him and the others from the end of their world.

The look of love and recognition on her face when she'd

had the vision of Laguz made his stomach turn. She had never once looked at him that way.

He pounded his fist on his desk, wishing that he could expend his anger in some destructive way. Why couldn't she see how perfect they were together? So what if Laguz was her Flame? Flames only got to be together at the end of the world, typically, so their unions were few and far between. Whereas he would always be there for her. Well, he always had been there for her, just not in the way he wanted to be.

Corduroy tried to calm his breathing, but could feel himself boiling. He decided to channel his anger into planning his next few classes on death.

The bloodier the better.

Chapter Five

Though he knew that it had not been Velvet's choice to have him as her assistant, her comment earlier had stung him. Linen had played the piece of music that was causing Velvet's vision, so that Tartan, the Professor of Human Culture, could identify it. Though he knew the name of it now, Linen still thought of it as 'Velvet's song'.

After playing, he'd made the mistake of telling Tartan that he was not an Old Soul, but a Faerie.

How was he supposed to know that Tartan hated Faeries? Or that he had been vying to help Velvet run the Academy? After Tartan had stormed off, Velvet had said that she would never in a million years choose Tartan to work with her.

So, out of curiosity, Linen had asked if she would have had him as her assistant, given the choice. And she had said no.

He couldn't help but feel a little hurt. He thought he had been doing a really good job, and was doing his best not to be irritating. Which for a Faerie, took an awful lot of concentration. He shifted around on his bed, but he couldn't get comfortable again.

Perhaps he should go for a walk instead. It was better than this false rest that he tried to get each night. He got up and walked slowly to the door. He made his way through the Academy to the gardens, and because it was the emptiest, decided to stay in the Underwater Garden. It was peaceful in the waterless current. He felt his body ebbing and flowing with the invisible tide, as though he really were at the bottom of the ocean. A fish swam lazily past him, making him smile. It had been a good idea, coming here, he felt better already.

He found some large smooth pebbles to sit on, and closed his eyes, listening to the water around him.

He breathed deeply and released his hurt, frustration and loneliness. Instead, he tried to focus on more positive things. He had missed out on greeting the Synapsian Starpeople earlier, and despite their ability to induce headaches, he was looking forward to meeting them. Velvet had warned him of her mistake, so he would endeavour to be more careful with his thoughts when he encountered one.

Voices floated towards him, muffled by the water, awakening him from his meditation. He opened his eyes and looked up to see an Angel in lilac coloured robes and a small green Faerie having a heated discussion.

Linen couldn't hear what they were saying, so he closed his eyes and resumed his meditation. A few moments later, the voices faded away and he was alone again.

When he felt completely calm and relaxed, he made his way back to his room, and resolved to spend the next few days focussing on his mission, on the new developments at the Academy and not worrying about what others thought of him. Perhaps avoiding Tartan would be a good idea too.

*   *   *

A frown on his face, Leon looked around him. How had he managed to take a wrong turn? The corridor he hovered in was unfamiliar, he was certain it hadn't been there before. Why would it have just popped up? He heard some voices behind him, and he turned to see who was coming. Perhaps he could ask them for directions.

The sight that greeted him when he turned around was so familiar, his jaw dropped open. He flew upwards and out of the way, and the crowd of human-looking Earth Angels that passed by beneath him didn't even notice him there as they passed by.

It was just like his vision, where he had Seen souls with human bodies and otherworldly origins. They were not trainees. So what were they doing at the Academy? Before he could decide if it was a good idea to speak to them, they had gone by, all heading in the same direction. He turned and followed them quietly, interested to see where they were going. When they reached the main hallway, Leon regained his bearings.

They all filed into the main hall, and Leon squeezed through the door last, hovering quietly at the back.

His eyes widened when Velvet took to the stage, and opened her arms in greeting.

"Welcome to the first class, MorningStars! I hope you have had time to settle in and relax, please, take a seat, and we will begin with some introductions. Though considering the size of the group, they will have to be very short I'm afraid."

She then asked if anyone had any questions, and a former Faerie called Delis said that she had told some trainees that she was a second-year, when put on the spot as to whom she was. Leon frowned when Velvet said that it would be a perfect explanation for their presence.

So Velvet didn't have a real explanation for them being there? How odd.

Leon waited until the beings were all noisily introducing themselves to one another before slipping out of the door unnoticed. He was late for his morning class now, so he flew speedily along the corridors until he reached Professor Indigo's room. He hoped the professor wouldn't be too annoyed by his lateness, though the Professor of Human Emotions always seemed to be annoyed.

He entered the classroom, and found half of his North America classmates all laughing hysterically, and the other half sobbing. He quickly joined the laughing half while Professor Indigo was facing away from them, intently writing something on the board.

He let himself be taken by the infectious giggling, and for the moment, forgot all of the puzzling events of the morning so far.

*   *   *

Corduroy's anger at himself, and his irritation with Laguz had lessened somewhat, after several classes of explosions, fire and darkness. Somehow, it was the darkness that brightened his mood, rather than the light. When surrounded by death and pain and anger, he would find himself feeling hopeful that things could get better. It was an odd kind of psychology, and sometimes he wondered whether he was just wired up wrong.

Corduroy tapped his fingers on his desk, and with a sigh he opened the drawer and pulled out a photograph he kept hidden there. He smoothed his thumb over it, and stared at the image.

Though he could manifest anything he wanted here, the only thing he had desperately wanted when he had arrived at the Academy was a photograph that he had treasured in one of his many lives. So he had manifested it. He looked down at her young face, a smile bringing out her dimples. She looked so happy. She was staring directly at the camera, and though the black and white image didn't show it, Corduroy knew that in that lifetime she'd been blonde, with deep green eyes. He looked at his own face, turned sideways away from the camera. He had been so busy staring at her, that he hadn't even noticed that his mother was taking their picture. Which was why he was a bit blurry. The old cameras had needed a very long exposure.

He sighed. Their life had been so simple then. They'd lived in a rural area, had spent most of their lives outside, and had been very happy. They had been best friends, though Corduroy had always hoped that one day they would become more. But they hadn't had the chance. Corduroy's hand shook as he tried not to remember that day that had scarred his soul and he touched her face once more before replacing the photograph in the drawer. He couldn't think about that day. It hurt too much.

Instead, he decided that it was time to call in for that raincheck with Velvet. Though he had a feeling that he already knew what she was going to say, he wanted to hear it from her.

He clicked his fingers and reappeared outside her office door. He knocked softly, but there was silence. Wanting to surprise her, he clicked his fingers and reappeared in her empty office. He saw Linen's desk for the first time, and went over to it. His disgust for the red-haired, orange-eyed freak reared up, and he rifled through some of the papers on the desk, half hoping to find something incriminating so that he could get him thrown out of the Academy. He hated to think of how closely he got to work with Velvet every day.

Finding nothing of interest, Corduroy wandered over to the other new addition to the office, a white grand piano. He hadn't played in many lifetimes, but the knowledge was still there. He sat on the stool and as soon as his fingers rested on the keys, they knew what to do. He knew no lullabies or soft melodies, he knew only how to play what called to him.

The harsh tones emanated from the piano, echoing around the room and enveloping him in his own pain and anger and frustration.

It wasn't until he had finished, and the last note faded

away, that he looked up and saw Velvet there, watching him. He felt so much lighter in her presence. "Hey." He got up from the stool and moved towards her, hoping for something to ease his internal aching. "I didn't know you had a piano, what have you been playing?"

Though the hug was brief, the touch of her skin against his, the smell of her silky, soft white hair, and the feel of her velvet robes under his hands was just enough to sustain him for a little longer.

*   *   *

It didn't surprise Mica that they were unsuccessful in finding the Leprechaun Garden. He found it incredibly difficult to concentrate on the many riddles and games they had to play to be granted the password. He looked at Emerald as they sat in the quiet of the Angelic Garden, and his heart felt heavy. Despite his declaration of confidence that the Flames would be reunited, and that the Awakening would occur, he still felt a needling of doubt about their own future together. He tried hard to hide it; he didn't want to project his feelings of gloom onto his Flame.

Why did he feel this oppressive negativity surrounding their reunion on Earth? It made no sense. If the Flames were being reunited, and everything was progressing towards the spiritual shift, then there should be no doubt that they would be together.

He thought of his last lifetime on Earth. The pain of being alone, of trying to have relationships with souls who were not Emerald, was so hard for him. He had yearned for her, longed for her, even though in that incarnation he had no conscious knowledge of who he was pining for. He didn't stay on Earth too long that time. It just hadn't felt right. When he had arrived on the Other Side, it had all become crystal clear to him. He understood the reasons for the feelings of loss and abandonment. As he was being asked the Ultimate Question, he had felt her presence behind him.

She had launched herself into his arms, and they had not let go of one another since.

He understood that they had not met in that lifetime because the Flames were not being reunited at that point in time, but he was still anxious that history may repeat itself and they may not meet again in the next.

"I know we will find each other. I will not rest until I am with you."

Mica smiled at Emerald, unsurprised that she had felt and understood his melancholy. He closed his eyes and nodded. "I know."

"Then let go of your fears, don't let them steal the joy of our time here, in this beautiful place."

Her words struck a chord with him, and a tear slid down his cheek. He felt Emerald's soft hand brush the tear away and he leaned into her embrace. "I love you, Emerald."

"As I love you, Mica. Always."

*　　　*　　　*

"Linen! You have come back at the perfect time. I have just put a call out to the other professors to meet me. I have some important things to discuss with the whole staff. Are you available to attend?"

Linen nodded and moved to his desk to retrieve his notebook. For some reason it wasn't where he remembered, and so it took him a minute to find it. He tried to smile at Corduroy, the Professor of Death, but only managed a grimace. He still found the professor to be quite terrifying, despite being a member of staff himself.

"I shall see you later, Velvet." Corduroy rose from the chair, and left the office, grinning at Linen as he went past, but Linen wasn't looking.

"Before we go to the meeting, I must discuss something with you."

Linen looked up at Velvet and his heart started hammering at the seriousness of her words. He moved to her desk and sat in the chair that Corduroy had just left.

"What is it, Velvet?"

Velvet sighed and leaned back in her chair. "There have been some dramatic changes in the last few days, and I feel I must inform my staff of them. The biggest development, is that I have realised that I need to return to Earth."

Linen's eyes widened. This was it. It was all happening in the way the Faeries had predicted. He didn't say anything, but nodded for Velvet to continue.

"Which means I will need someone to run the Academy. Seeing as you have been studying the position, although only for a few days, admittedly, I feel it is only right that you are the one to take over." She shook her head to herself. "I never dreamt I would hand over my role to a Faerie, but as I am realising quite quickly, stranger things have happened."

Linen closed his gaping mouth and gulped. "Are you saying you actually want me to run this place?"

"Yes, Linen, as crazy as it may seem, considering all I have said about not wanting you here, I am."

"I see. Thank you. It means a lot to me that you think I can do this." Linen couldn't believe it. It seemed he was right to let go of his hurt before. Because it now she could see his true worth, and his capability to run the Academy.

"Yes, I do." Velvet stood up. "We had better get to the meeting. I have much work to do and this may take a while." She moved to the door and after a moment, Linen jumped up and followed her.

*   *   *

Corduroy went back to his office briefly before the meeting.

After Velvet had explained everything to him, he felt the need for a few moments alone to process it.

Velvet was going to Earth. She was leaving the Academy. And she would be leaving Linen in charge. Corduroy laughed out loud. She clearly wasn't interested in the red-headed freak then. Which was why he had smiled at Linen on the way out. He clearly wasn't a threat anymore, seeing as he wouldn't even be in the same dimension as Velvet soon.

But Corduroy would be. There was no way that he would stay here while Velvet left. He wanted to be on Earth with her again. Maybe this time they would finally be together. He knew that telling her about Laguz had been a mistake, but he wasn't going to let the fish get in-between them again. She would forget about Laguz, but she wouldn't be able to forget about Corduroy. He'd make sure that he found her.

He pulled out the photograph again, and this time put it in the inside pocket of his robes. He leaned back in his chair and closed his eyes. He pictured the two of them together in their next lifetime, finally having the relationship that he had been dreaming of for millennia.

It would be about time.

Chapter Six

"Thank you for making your way here to attend this gathering. I have some important news to share with you, news that will affect us all. I was visited by an Angel, who asked me if we would go to Earth."

The Crystal Child paused and looked around at the glowing, beautiful Children sitting around her in the quartz cave. One of them raised a hand and she nodded to the boy with obsidian black hair and eyes.

"But we are already on Earth. We are there in scores, how many more of us do they need?"

The Child shook her head. "She did not ask for us to go in our true form. She wishes for us to go and be born on Earth as humans."

There was a gasp from one of the Children, her amethyst eyes were wide in shock. "They want us to be human?" she whispered.

The quartz Crystal Child nodded. "Yes, that was her wish. She said that though our Crystal energy on Earth has helped to raise the vibration, we are needed there in human form to raise the vibration even further. I said that I didn't think our gentle energy would translate well into human beings, but she assured me that it would work. We will also receive some training at a School before we arrive on Earth."

This time there was excited whispering. With no need for

schooling in the Crystal World, it would be a new experience for all of them.

"It will not be easy. Their world is so different from ours. There is war and poverty and hate." The other Crystals were now looking at one another, worried. "But there is beauty there, too, and perhaps we can help the humans to see this beauty, and to focus on it, create more of it and perhaps even help them to experience the love and peace that we do here."

"Do we have to go?" a small girl with glimmering orange eyes asked.

"No. You can stay. I asked you all here, as representatives of each crystal family. You can choose to go, or you can ask others to go, or both, or neither. It is entirely your choice." She took a deep breath, and looked around the cave, a little sad. "I will be going. I wish to see for myself what it is like, and I wish to be of service."

There were a few nods of agreement. "When must we decide?" the amethyst Crystal Child asked.

"As soon as possible. It will take a little time to transport ourselves to the School in the Fifth Dimension, and the Angel said we should waste no time."

"I will go. And I will ask the other orange Crystals if they wish to go."

One by one, each different coloured Crystal Child agreed to go.

"We should all be represented," the boy with obsidian eyes said. "It is only fair."

"Thank you. I will make the preparations for our departure, and make sure that everything still runs smoothly here for when we one day return to our home."

"Is that even possible?"

"I do not know, Sister. But I hope that it is so."

*   *   *

It was really happening. Linen walked down the corridor towards room 333, hardly able to believe that everything that the Faeries had told him was coming true.

In the meeting, Velvet had explained to the staff that she would be going to Earth to help with the shift, and so she would be handing the Academy over to Linen. One by one, her staff declared they would go with her. She had started talking about replacing them, which was when Linen had stepped in.

He was still trembling slightly at the fact that he had addressed a room full of Old Souls. He still found them all quite intimidating, apart from Athena, of course. But then she was an Angel, not an Old Soul.

He had told them the whole story. Why he was there, what the Faeries had told him, and that he'd heard the Angel trying to save him and had ignored her pleas. He told them about his dream of the Angel with the star-studded wings, and how she asked him to return. Then he told them that it wouldn't be necessary to replace the staff with Old Souls, because the Academy would no longer be for Earth Angels. It would be for the Children of the Golden Age.

But still, even in the telling of his story, he doubted whether he was right, and whether any of it would happen.

Then right in the middle of the meeting, it did happen.

The Indigo Children arrived.

Velvet and Corduroy had already welcomed them, now Linen was on his way with Corduroy to meet them himself. He didn't know why the Professor of Death had made him walk the last couple of corridors, when Linen knew full well he could have used the Old Soul Magick to take them immediately to the door. Perhaps he was just trying to make him nervous. Which was unnecessary, Linen already felt queasy from being transported there. Linen looked sideways at Corduroy's face, surprised to see that for once, the gloomy professor looked quite cheerful.

When they arrived at the door, Corduroy gestured to it

with a flourish and it disappeared. A click later, he also disappeared, leaving Linen standing there by himself. He slowly walked into the room, unsure of what he would find. He stood in the darkness for a moment, until it occurred to him to manifest light. He gasped out loud at the sight of the magnificent Golden City that appeared before his eyes. It was as if an entire world existed within the classroom. It shimmered in the light he had manifested. But what he couldn't take his eyes off of were the blue spheres of light zooming around the city.

He stood in awe for a few minutes, then cleared his throat and called out, "Hello?"

The lights stopped moving at the sound of his voice, and they all zoomed towards him. He resisted the urge to step backwards, and smiled nervously instead. Once they got within a few feet, each sphere of blue light transformed into a beautiful Child. Linen bowed his head to them, feeling a surge of respect and love for these Children who had come from so far to help Earth.

"Welcome, Children. My name is Linen, and I will be the Head of the School for the Children of the Golden Age."

The Children all nodded back to him, and the smallest Child stepped forwards to speak.

"Hello, Linen. Thank you for coming to greet us. Velvet said you would."

"You are most welcome. I am so pleased to see you. How did you know to come here?"

"Starlight, the Angel, came to visit me. She explained that we were needed on Earth to help initiate the changes to bring about the Golden Age."

"Yes, I know the Angel you mean. She came to visit me and told me the same thing. That I was needed here, to help with the Children. I haven't recruited the teachers yet, or set a plan or anything, so I'm afraid I don't have classes for you all to attend just yet."

The Indigo Child smiled. "That's okay, we are quite happy to remain in our Golden City until you are ready. Do you know when you will be?"

"It will be as soon as I can get everything organised. I promise you will be the first to know when it is ready."

"Thank you, Linen, we look forward to seeing you again very soon."

Linen nodded and backed away, but just as he was about to turn towards the door, he noticed that all of the Children had turned back into lights and zoomed back to the city, except for the tiny girl who had spoken. She moved closer to him, a concerned look on her face.

"Linen, I have a question."

"Of course, what is it?"

She leaned in closer and Linen dropped to one knee to hear her better. "Do you think this is going to work?"

Linen frowned. "What do you mean? The School?"

"No, I mean the changes on Earth. Do you really think we can make that much of a difference?"

Linen saw his own insecurities reflected back to him in the Child's eyes. He realised that he needed to be a role model that the Children could look up to. It felt like a heavy responsibility for a Faerie like him, but he knew he needed to find his courage and be strong like Velvet.

He looked the Child directly in the eye and nodded. "Absolutely. I have complete faith in you and the other Children."

The Indigo Child smiled. "Thank you."

"You're welcome." Linen went to stand, but the Child held her hand out to him once more.

"I was told that one of the Indigos that left our world a very long time ago may be here. Would you know where I could find them?"

Linen shook his head. "I'm afraid I don't know of any Indigos here, I could ask Velvet though. She will know."

The Child nodded. "Yes, please do. I should very much like to see them again."

"I will do my best."

With that, the Child turned into a blue sphere and zoomed away. Linen took one last look at the Golden City then left the room. He stood outside in the hallway for a few moments just trying to process all that had happened, and all that was about to occur.

*   *   *

"Good evening, Linen," Velvet greeted him as he entered the office.

Linen went to his desk and sat down. For once, he couldn't find the words to reply.

"Are you okay?" Velvet peered at him, concerned. "You look a little strange."

Linen shook his head. "I'm fine. Just feeling a bit overwhelmed right now. Is this all really happening?"

Velvet sighed. "Yes it is. And I agree, it is quite overwhelming. I cannot believe all that has happened in a mere few days since the beginning of term." She looked around the office. "I felt sure that this was where I would spend my time for the foreseeable future. I never once imagined that I would return to Earth."

Linen blinked and focused on the Old Soul. She had the same look on her face as the other day when he had played the piano. He hadn't asked her if she knew why she reacted so strongly when she heard the song. But he figured it must have something to do with a past life, and now that she was returning to Earth, a future life, too.

He sighed. His mind was just whirring with everything that needed to be done. It was difficult to concentrate. The words of the Indigo Child flashed into his head.

"Velvet, do you know of any Indigos here at the

Academy? One of the Children seemed to think that there was one here."

Velvet smiled. "Well yes, I believe that Indigo Batik, the Professor of Human Emotions, originated from the Indigo World."

Linen raised his eyebrows. "How come he didn't say anything? Didn't he know they were coming?"

Velvet shook her head. "It's been so long since he left their world, his connection with them has been long since lost. He doesn't like to speak of it."

"That's sad."

"Well, perhaps now that his brothers and sisters are here, he will open up about it."

"Yes, perhaps."

Linen was silent for a while. Now his mind was whirring even more. He just couldn't imagine how he would get anything done.

"Would you mind if I played for a while?" he asked Velvet, gesturing to the piano.

Velvet bit her lip. "Not at all, I will have to go shortly, but please, enjoy."

Linen nodded and moved to the piano stool. He began the opening notes of the song and out of the corner of his eye, he saw Velvet rise from her chair and quietly leave the office.

He played until all of his thoughts were in order, until he felt relaxed, and then his hands became still.

"Starlight, please help me," he whispered. "I'm in over my head. Help me."

*   *   *

Starlight smiled at Linen's prayer. He was coping wonderfully, even if he lacked faith and belief in himself. She had been watching the trainees at the Academy, and she knew that help would soon be coming his way; it was not necessary for her to step in this time. She just hoped he would be patient.

She watched the progress of the Crystal Children as they travelled through the Universe to the Academy. It would not be too long before they arrived, and the changes would begin in earnest.

Chapter Seven

When Laguz opened his eyes and saw Velvet sat on the bench in front of him, humming their song, he couldn't believe it. She had called to him. And that call had reached through the dimensions to where he was working as a guide. In an instant, he answered the call, and found himself in what looked like their garden from their lifetime in Atlantis. He stepped towards her and a movement caught his eye. He looked up to see an Angel stood just beyond the archway of the garden and he winked at her. She held her hand up as if to apologise and flew away.

He approached Velvet quietly. Her eyes were closed and she was still humming. She looked the same as the last time he had seen her, white hair, soft wrinkles. But she didn't look as frail. She looked wise and powerful, and even more beautiful than his memory of her. Had it really been so long since they were last together? Why had she called him now? He had missed her so deeply for so long.

When he was just a step away from her, he couldn't stay quiet any longer. "Velvet, my love."

*   *   *

A short while later, Laguz lay in bed alongside Velvet and watched her rest. All that had happened before the moment he had taken her into his arms for the first time in several ages, faded into the background. Though he had been waiting for her call for a very long time, nothing mattered but being there with her now.

He gently stroked her long hair, careful not to disturb her. Within minutes of their reunion, it had become dark and glossy, and her face had become smooth and youthful. She looked just as she had in Atlantis before the end.

His heart clenched and his vision blurred. Though it was such a long time ago now, it still broke his heart to recall the moment she breathed for the last time in his arms. Leaving her empty shell there on the beach was the hardest thing he had ever had to do. And if he had known that it would be the last time he would hold her for thousands of years, he may have held on just a few moments longer.

Just then, Velvet opened her eyes and looked up at him. She smiled, and his heart healed, becoming whole again.

*   *   *

Leon was listening intently to Velvet during the meeting she had called for the entire Academy. He was only a little surprised when she arrived at the meeting late looking like a much younger version of herself. He had seen her looking like that before, in one of his visions.

She told them they would have to accelerate their training, which meant they would be getting their human bodies soon. Though Leon would be sad he would not fit in his tiny toadstool hideaway any longer, he had fully accepted that being here at the Academy meant that he would lose his wings. He was actually quite curious, and weirdly looking forward to having a human body for the first time.

Partway through the meeting, the side door opened and an Old Soul entered and sat in the front row. Leon followed his movements and found he was unable to look away. He knew this soul. He had seen him several times before in his visions, but had not understood who he was. He watched the silent interaction between the soul and Velvet when she mentioned Twin Flames, and understood instantly that was what they were. He tore his gaze away and took his notebook out. He flipped through the pages until he reached the vision he'd had of himself travelling around in a bus-like vehicle. The sketch of his companion looked exactly like the Old Soul in the front row with long blond hair. Interesting.

Having taken in only some of the rest of the information shared by Velvet, (the most important parts being that she was returning to Earth, the Flames were being reunited and that the Children of the Golden Age had arrived) Leon allowed himself to be moved along by the chattering crowd as they left the main hall. He ended up flying behind Aria and her Angel friend, Amethyst.

"It's weird that she didn't mention that the Children arrived in such a cool golden city, it looked amazing," Aria said.

"I suppose she didn't want everyone rushing over to look. It would be a bit overwhelming for the Children, I should think." Amethyst replied in her soft voice.

Leon watched the Faerie's wings droop a little as they flew in front of him. "Am, I really don't think I'm ready to lose my wings. Must we really become human this afternoon?"

"It will be alright, Aria. You knew that it would be happening at some point. At the rate things are changing, it would be best to get it over with now, to give us time to adjust to being human."

Aria sighed and her wings drooped even lower. "I guess."

"Why don't we go to the gardens for a while, and enjoy our wings while we have them?"

Leon watched Aria perk up a little, and challenge Amethyst to a race. As they sped off towards the gardens, Leon too, wondered whether to spend the last of his time as a Faerie in the toadstool house. But instead, he found himself flying back to his room. He had spent very little time there, so he thought it best to get used to being there more. As soon as the door disappeared he heard the unheavenly screeching of Coral, the Mermaid.

He winced and wondered if her vocals would improve at all once she was human. He really hoped so. He flew back down the corridor, at a loss of where to go. He had kept to himself so much that he had made no friends, and barely knew his classmates.

Deciding to go to the gardens after all, he flew to the Atlantis Garden, and found it curiously empty. He sat on a bench that seemed to face a gap in the golden statues, and took out his notebook.

He found his sketch of the city, the one made entirely of gold, and wondered if it looked like the city the Children had arrived in. He found a few more sketches of the blond Old Soul, and wondered again how he would end up friends with him. Leon had been fairly insignificant in the Elemental Realm; he had not had a position of authority or nobility, and aside from the usefulness of his ability to See danger or bad weather coming, he was a nobody.

To think that he may become close to two souls who were bound to be instrumental in the massive spiritual Awakening on Earth, scared him a little. Was he going to be an important part of it all too? Leon took a deep breath and tucked his notebook away. Though he had decided to come to the Academy because he wanted to go to Earth to make a difference, the responsibility of having a significant role in the Awakening was overwhelming to him. He squared his small shoulders and straightened his wings. He hoped that when he had a human body, it would seem more manageable.

Because right now, Leon felt too small to be able to change anything at all.

*   *   *

After the big meeting with all of the staff, trainees and second-years, Linen went back to the office alone. He still couldn't believe the change in Velvet. She looked about fifty years younger. He realised now why she was returning to Earth. She was going to be with her Twin Flame again.

He had heard of Twin Flames, but he didn't really understand what all the fuss was about. Besides, he had more pressing things to worry about, such as learning how to run a School. He glanced at Velvet's empty desk. She had disappeared off with Laguz immediately after the meeting. He got a feeling he wouldn't be seeing much of her from now on.

Yet again he found himself unable to concentrate, so he set his notes down, and decided to pay the Indigos a visit.

He walked to room 333, and resolved to ask Velvet again to teach him the Old Soul Magick. He wanted to be able to click his fingers and move to wherever he wanted to go. It was much more convenient.

He entered the room, lighting it with his thoughts. He called out his presence to the blue lights in the Golden City.

One of them came shooting over to him, and transformed into the blonde Child just a few steps away.

"You have found them?" she asked excitedly.

Linen nodded. "I asked Velvet, and she told me it was one of the professors. But she said that he did not like to speak of his origins, and that he had lost connection with you after so many years of being away. So I am not sure he will want to meet you."

The Child frowned for a second, then her face lit up again. "Can I at least try? Would you take me to him?"

Linen nodded. "I can't see the harm in that. Follow me, I will take you to his office."

"Thank you, Linen." She turned to the city and sent the thought to her siblings that she would return shortly, then followed Linen from the room. It was the first time she had seen any of the Academy other than room 333, and her eyes were wide as they walked through the corridors. When they reached Professor Indigo's office, Linen knocked and the door disappeared.

The professor looked up at Linen and gave him a half-smile. "Hello, Linen. What can I do for you?"

"I have someone here who wishes to see you." Linen waved the Indigo Child forwards, from where she was hiding behind him.

The professor's eyes widened when he saw her.

"Hello, Indigo," she said.

Linen stepped back towards the door. "I will leave you to talk. If you need my assistance in getting back to your city, just call me."

The Indigo Child nodded. "Thank you, Linen."

Linen left the office and headed back to his. He could no longer procrastinate, it was time to plan his School.

*　　　*　　　*

"Oh, Indigo Child," the professor whispered. "It's so good to see you." He stood up from his chair and crossed the room to where she stood.

She opened her arms and he fell to his knees and hugged her hard.

"I have missed you, lost Indigo. When your connection was severed so long ago, I thought I would never see you again."

"I thought the same." The professor pulled back and the Child lifted her hand to his face to wipe away his tears.

"Do not cry, I just wish to understand how you became cut off from us? It's just that I am afraid that if we all go to Earth, we shall become cut off from our home and from each other, too."

The professor stood and led the Child by the hand to his

desk. He helped her into a chair that was far too big for her, and pulled his own chair around his desk to sit next to her.

"I'm sure you won't lose your connection. I think I lost mine because I had so many human lives. The more lives I had, the further from home I became. I lost hope that I would ever be able to return."

"You could have returned. You could have resumed your true form and travelled the Universe back to us."

"I forgot the way," the professor whispered. "I began to believe I was simply human. Though at times, I am sure I dreamt of flying home and being in the Golden City once more." He smiled, this time a genuine smile. "Seeing you has brought back all of those memories, and makes me miss it even more."

"How would you like to visit?"

Professor Indigo frowned. "I'm not sure I understand?"

The Indigo Child hopped off the chair and held her hand out to him. "Let me show you."

He followed the Child to room 333 in silence. And when the room lit up and he saw the city, the tears began to run freely down his face.

"You can still change, you know. Just set your intention to return home. Then you will resume your true form." With those words, she transformed herself back into a sphere of blue light, and zoomed towards the city to join her siblings. The professor watched for a while, then he closed his eyes, and quietly repeated: "I wish to return home," three times. As he uttered the word 'home' for the third time, he felt his body changing and morphing. Though uncomfortable at first, he soon found himself to be free for the first time in millennia. When he opened his awareness again, he found that he was a pure sphere of Indigo light. His true form. He moved towards the city slowly, taking in its beauty. Then once within the city walls, he was overwhelmed by the connection he experienced with his fellow Indigos.

They surrounded him in a joyful dance, and their spirited thoughts lifted him higher and higher, making him feel the happiest he had ever been.

He was finally home.

*   *   *

If Corduroy had been feeling violent before, his mood was now so black that he felt like bringing a black plague upon Earth. Maybe on the rest of the Universe too.

Laguz was back. For the first time since Atlantis, he was with Velvet again. Corduroy paced up and down his office, his brown robes flicking back and forth.

Just when he thought he had a chance! Just when he had finally decided to come clean and tell Velvet how he felt, that old fish had come back.

Corduroy wanted to scream and shout but knew it would make no difference.

He threw himself into his chair and closed his eyes. He knew he needed to control his anger, to rein in his rage, so that he didn't say or do anything he would regret for eternity. And he knew there was only one way he could do that.

For the first time in many lifetimes, he allowed himself to go back to that moment. That hideous moment that had damaged his soul for many lifetimes afterwards.

He could still smell the salty brine on the breeze. He could still feel the sand between his toes, grinding into his flesh with every step forwards. He had decided not to become a Merperson, he had decided to remain in Atlantis, and allow its fate to be his.

As he approached the water's edge, his heart clenched painfully and each step became unbearable. When he saw her closed eyes, her white hair and her beautiful face, aged beyond recognition, he stumbled and fell.

He crawled the last few feet until he reached her lifeless

body, not caring that the waves were lapping at his feet, soaking into the hems of his trousers. He touched her cold cheek and a sob escaped from him, ripping out his heart. Tears now streaming down his face, he gathered her up into his arms and buried his face in her hair.

In that moment, he resolved never to love so deeply again, but to shut down his feelings and focus on destruction instead. When the world ended, he welcomed the darkness.

Corduroy opened his eyes, and the memory faded. He didn't bother to wipe away the tears running down his cheek. The memory of the moment was as painful as the moment itself had been, but it served its purpose in calming him. He had never managed to harden himself enough to block out the love he felt for Velvet. It had remained true and strong and at times, overwhelming. But if he focused on the darker side, on death and pain, then he was able to cope with the fact that his love had never been reciprocated.

Corduroy breathed deeply, until his rage had completely subsided. He knew that he would have to tolerate the fact that Laguz was there, and with Velvet, but he also knew that it would not be an easy task. It required staying away from Velvet as much as possible, and he also hoped he did not come face to face with Laguz.

Because if he did, he knew he would do something he would regret.

Chapter Eight

Linen was whistling a tune happily to himself as he entered the office, only to be stopped in his tracks by the scene in front of him.

"Oh! Uh, Linen, sorry about that, um, just a second."

Linen averted his eyes. "I'm sorry. I should have, erm, knocked, or something."

Velvet laughed as she straightened herself up. "Oh, don't be silly, this is your office as well, there's no need to knock."

Linen risked looking upwards and was relieved to see both Velvet and her Flame looking presentable again.

"I don't think we've met properly yet," Laguz said, stepping forwards. "I'm Laguz." He held his hand out, and Linen shook it. Linen tried not to openly stare at his bare chest that was on display through his almost translucent shirt.

"Linen. Nice to meet you, Laguz." He dragged his gaze up to Laguz's green eyes and nodded.

Laguz looked at Velvet, who was still flushed, her dark hair in disarray. "Shall we?" he asked, holding his hand out. Velvet grinned and took it. With a click of her fingers, they were gone.

Linen sighed and went over to his desk. He still hadn't had the chance to ask Velvet all the questions he needed answering about the finer details of running an Academy. But he figured he wouldn't be getting much sense out of her, as long as Laguz was around.

He sat quietly for a moment, and took a deep breath. He was still completely overwhelmed with everything that he needed to do. Every time he tried to comprehend the bigger picture, he felt like running away, or, if he could get his wings back, flying away – as fast as possible.

But he could just focus on one thing at a time. That seemed possible. And the first thing he needed to do was to recruit some new teachers. Soon, there wouldn't be anyone left here but him, as the staff were all following Velvet to Earth. So he would need to recruit a team of teachers to help him with the Children. But he had already been told by the Faeries that Old Souls weren't the right kind of teachers. He would need to hire Angels and Faeries. Lighter beings, who could help the Children understand the human world, but not get dragged down by the heaviness of the denser energy.

Linen looked up at the wall and called out Beryl's name three times. She was Velvet's secretary, and had already said that she would help him in any way she could.

"Yes, Linen?" Beryl's kind, Angelic face appeared on the wall.

"I need to recruit new teachers from the Angelic Realm and Elemental Realm for the School. Do you know how I go about doing this?"

"Of course, Linen. Your first port of call should be the recruitment souls, you will find them in their office, three doors down. They will be able to help you with any promotional materials you need. They will also help you with interviewing and hiring tips."

Linen nodded. "Yes, of course. Because we never see or hear anything from them, I forget they actually exist."

"They do like to keep to themselves. You will rarely see them outside of their office."

"Thank you, Beryl," Linen said, standing up. "I shall go there right now. At least then I will feel as though I have made a start."

"Everything will be just great, Linen. I have total faith in you, no matter what others might say."

Linen winced and remembered Tartan's reaction to the news of him taking over the Academy.

Beryl faded from the wall and Linen made his way to the recruitment office. Though he had previously passed the door on the way to his own room, he had taken very little notice of it.

He knocked and the door disappeared. He had only taken one step inside when his jaw dropped.

It looked nothing like a normal office. There were no desks or chairs, no pens or notebooks.

Instead, it was a large white room with giant screens lining one wall. The screens were a mass of images and words, being moved around at high speeds by the Faeries in front of them. Linen tried to follow their movements but ended up feeling dizzy. On the other side of the room, there were several Angels who looked like they were in deep meditation.

After several moments, Linen was aware of a glowing being moving towards him. He frowned, wondering why there was a Starperson trainee in the recruitment office. As if in answer to his thoughts, a few feet away, the being turned into a tall, skinny man with brown hair and blue eyes.

"Welcome, Linen. How can we help you?"

"I know you, you're Bk, right?"

Bk nodded. "Yes I am, we met when the Zubenelgenubi and the Pyrydian Starpeople arrived."

"I didn't realise you could still assume your true form." Linen glanced over his shoulder. "Do you think I could still be a Faerie sometimes?"

Bk smiled. "Possibly. Though it has taken me several decades to perfect the art of switching between the two. The only reason I switch is so that I can more easily communicate with other planets. I also think a lot better when in my true form. My human thoughts and feelings get in the way of true creativity, I find."

Linen felt a little disappointed; he had hoped he would be able to have his wings back every now and then.

"Anyway, the reason I am here, is to ask for your help and expertise in recruiting Angels and Faeries for the new School for the Children of the Golden Age. I assume you have heard of their arrival by now?"

Bk nodded. "Yes, of course, we know everything that happens around here. We were waiting for you to come and visit. Where are you wanting to recruit teachers from?"

"The Angelic and Elemental Realms."

"Okay, let's see what we can come up with." Bk turned and called out to a Faerie with luminous pink dragonfly wings. "Dahlia, could you help us out here? We need to create the brochures for the new School."

Dahlia flew over from her screen and nodded excitedly. "Yes, of course. Come over to my screen, and we will create it together." She grinned at Linen, then zoomed back over to her screen. Linen and Bk followed at a slower pace. The Faerie began by wiping clean everything that she had been working on, then very quickly, began to build up words and images of the Academy that could be used for the new brochures. Linen watched her in fascination, forgetting that he was there to contribute. He started calling out suggestions, and then filling in details of how the School would be run.

He still felt a bit overwhelmed, even with the help he was receiving. As the brochure took shape, the idea of running the entire School began to make him feel a little faint. He was just a Faerie, he didn't have any experience with anything like this.

For the second time, in his mind, he pleaded with Starlight. Surely she would help him out?

*   *   *

Starlight shook her head. It was funny how impatient Faeries could be! She wondered if she should inform Linen that help was indeed on the way, but then if he expected her to warn him every time something was about to happen, she would spend every moment visiting him, and not get on with her real job, which was orchestrating the events of the entire Universe.

It amused Starlight how people on Earth believed that a deity called God ruled the Universe. Though he did play a big part, he really only looked after Earth. Starlight was the one who oversaw the rest of it. She realised in that moment that it had been some time since she had visited. She closed her eyes and thought of him.

*   *   *

"Do you think that looks right, Professor?"

Corduroy blinked at the Mermaid, who was timidly asking his opinion of her newly formed human body. He glanced at it and saw it was quite plain, but then the Mermaid herself wasn't much to look at. He nodded.

"Yes, yes, that's great." He left her to assume the form and found himself glancing back over to where Velvet was helping her group to transform. He wished he hadn't snapped at her earlier. The look of hurt and confusion on her face had hurt him also. But when she had floated in, looking young and radiant and so much in love, he had felt something die inside.

Why couldn't he make her feel that way? He was sure he could, if she gave him the chance to. That's all he was really wanted, just one chance. Was it really so much to ask?

Velvet's group erupted into laughter then, and Corduroy snapped at his group to pay attention to their own transformations and not get distracted by the others. Not that he was really paying attention himself, but he didn't feel in the mood to let his trainees have fun.

By the time the last soul in his groups had been

transformed, Corduroy's foot was aching from his impatient tapping. The trainees all left the main hall, now slowly and sedately, trying to get used to their heavy new bodies. He watched them leave, then looked up to see Velvet watching him, a slight frown on her face. She opened her mouth, but before she could say a word, Corduroy clicked his fingers and left, reappearing in the dark gloom of his office. He slammed his fist down onto his desk, and was briefly thankful that it wasn't possible to break bones in this dimension.

He knew he was being cowardly. But if he had stayed another moment in her presence, he would have confessed everything. And on top of everything else right now, her rejection was something that he just could not face.

No, best for him to just stay here, in his own little space, in the dark, and wait until he felt ready to be around others again. He fell into his chair and clutched his hand to his chest, where the photograph was tucked away in his pocket.

Despite everything, he still could not give up. He would never give up.

*　　*　　*

Leon left the main hall that afternoon, his new body feeling stiff and weird to him. Each step he took seemed to echo through the hallway. He was not used to making so much noise. His fluttering wings created only a whisper, but now his huge feet made him sound like a giant was passing through.

It was so odd to be so tall! Though he was used to flying up over everyone's heads when he needed to, touching the ground yet still seeing above people's heads at the same time was the oddest experience ever.

His thoughts flitted to the tiny green Faerie, Aria. He was glad in a way that she had freaked out after he had been changed into a human, otherwise he might have felt panicked too. He hoped that Velvet and Amethyst were able to calm her, and to help her. If only she realised that being human wasn't so bad. It was heavier, yes, but it wasn't bad. But then he figured that he may begin to miss flying after a while. He walked slowly to the gardens, thinking that he would need to allow more time to get to his classes from now on; feet were a lot slower than wings.

He went to the Elemental Garden and was amazed at how small everything looked. He knelt down on one knee and peered underneath the toadstool, to see the tiny door underneath. He couldn't believe that up until just a few hours ago, he had fit in there. His eyes widened as a thought suddenly occurred to him. He patted the pockets of his shirt and trousers until he found a small rectangular bump. He pulled out the tiny notebook and sighed in relief. He should have left it behind in his room, what if it had disappeared with his Faerie body during the transformation? His big and unwieldy fingers struggled to flip the pages, and he decided to see if he could get a bigger notebook. Manifestation was a much slower process now, as they had to learn how humans coped without being able to manifest things instantly. So Leon got up, tucked the tiny notebook safely in his shirt pocket and headed out of the gardens towards the classrooms. Hopefully he would be able to get a notebook from one of the professors.

As he left the gardens, he had a vision of himself in the Atlantis Garden, and without fully thinking it through, found himself diverting his course to the path that led to the jewelled garden. When he reached the archway entrance, his pace slowed and he found himself stepping as lightly as he could, making as little noise as possible. He saw the blond Old Soul sat on the bench and his breath caught. Why did he feel like this in his presence? It was a cross between fear and excitement and something else. He swallowed as he realised that the last feeling he had was something like attraction. The blond Old Soul's energy was magnetic to him. Leon considered announcing his presence and speaking to the soul, after all, why not? But his heavy feet stayed stuck to the ground, and Leon silently watched the soul instead, as he appeared to be deep in thought.

Chapter Nine

Laguz was sat in the Atlantis Garden, his eyes blind to the sparkle of the jewels around him. It had been so long since he had allowed himself to think about Velvet. He had closed off his memories of her, of their lives together, for several ages. Seeing her again, breathing her scent, hearing her voice, it had brought everything rushing back to him, like a tidal wave that was trying to drown him.

He closed his eyes and saw Velvet in their home in Atlantis, standing by the glass windows that faced the beach. It was the middle of the night, and she was just staring out into the inky darkness. He had woken up and found her gone from the bed, and he remembered coming up behind her, and wrapping his arms around her. He put his head on her shoulder, and when his cheek had touched hers, he realised it was wet.

"What is it?" he whispered.

She was silent for a while, and all Laguz could hear were the waves crashing on the rocks. "I had a dream."

"Was it a bad one?" Both of them being Seers, prophetic dreams were fairly typical, but he hadn't seen her so upset about one before.

She nodded, and more tears flowed down her cheeks. He tightened his grip. "Tell me about it." He waited patiently until she managed to utter the words.

"I had a vision, yesterday, of the end of our world," she whispered. Laguz stiffened and his heart started to thump loudly.

"So I prayed before sleep, to be given a solution, to save our people."

Laguz swallowed. "Did you dream of a solution?"

Velvet nodded, her jaw tight. "Yes. I did."

Laguz sighed in relief. "So there is a way to avoid this fate?"

"For most, yes."

Laguz frowned and stood straight, turning Velvet around so he could look her in the eye. Her tear-stained face was lit only by the candlelight that spilled out from their bedroom. "What do you mean, for most?"

Velvet met his gaze, her expression pained. "For you. You will be saved."

"But not you?" Laguz's heart stopped.

Velvet shook her head. "Nor our child." She rested her hand on the barely visible bump under her nightgown.

Laguz felt tears running down his face, soaking his shirt. They had been trying to conceive for many years, without success and they were so excited that they were finally going to be parents.

"How long?"

"Within the next two months. Just enough time to ensure your safety, and the safety of our people."

Laguz frowned. "I don't understand. If there is time to prepare, why can you not come too? Can we not plan for your safety?"

Velvet shook her head. "The world will not exist as we know it now. It will all soon be underwater. In my dream, I was told that the only way you can survive is to become people of the sea, to live on the ocean bed."

Laguz shook his head. "That sounds crazy."

Velvet gave him a half-smile. "I know, but the dream was

vivid and clear. I was given the incantation to turn you all into sea people."

"But not to turn yourself into one too?"

"It is my understanding that it takes a lot of energy to perform these transformations, and once I have changed all of those who wish to go, I will have used up every bit of energy I have."

By now Laguz was shaking. Though he was trying to be rational and calm, his heart was screaming in pain. He couldn't lose her. He couldn't lose his child, not after waiting for so long. Yet he trusted Velvet's visions. They were very rarely inaccurate. A thought suddenly occurred to him.

"What if you show me the incantation? I could change people too, then we'd have enough energy between us to change each other and we could go together."

More tears ran down Velvet's cheeks. "I wish that were possible, but only I have the power to do this."

"How do you know?" Laguz could hear the desperation in his own voice, and had to refrain from shaking her shoulders.

"I just do. You do not have the power to create these transformations. Only I do." She stepped forwards and kissed him deeply, and he kissed her back, his tears mingling with hers on their cheeks. He kissed her more passionately than he ever had before, and she responded by melting into his arms. He felt the warmth of her skin through her nightgown as she pressed up against him. He pulled back a little.

"Must you do anything tonight?"

She shook her head and allowed him to lead her back to the bedroom, where they spent the rest of the night in each other's arms, dreading the dawning of the new day.

Laguz opened his eyes. Tears were streaming down his cheeks as the pain of losing not only Velvet, but his child as well, came surging through the ages until it hit him squarely in the chest. He dropped his head into his hands and his body shook. He couldn't go through that pain again. Yet somehow, he knew that it was inevitable. He prayed that if he and Velvet managed to meet on Earth, and were together once again, that he would be taken first. But then he didn't wish for Velvet to suffer the loss of him either. Perhaps they could be taken together. He thought about whether he should have reminded Velvet about their child. About how she had miscarried after she had done the first few transformations. She had been devastated, and it had taken a huge amount of courage and strength to continue her mission. She had changed after the loss. She had resigned herself to her fate and given up hope.

Laguz figured if he had told her, reminded her of these facts that she had long forgotten, it would stir up that feeling of hopelessness once more. Besides that, he found it extremely difficult to talk about it. In all the ages since Atlantis, in all the lives he had lived since then, he had never had children.

He was so lost in his memories and musings that he didn't properly register it the first time. But the second time, it was a little louder, and unmistakeable.

He was being called.

"No," he whispered. "I'm not ready to leave her yet." As if in response to his pleas, he heard the Angelic voice again and he sighed.

After spending the last six ages without her, after nearly being destroyed by their separation last time, it seemed cruel that the Universe would give him a mere few days with his love before tearing them apart once more.

He knew that Velvet had a meeting this afternoon, so he didn't want to bother her, but he also knew that he needed to spend as much time as possible in her embrace before answering the Angel's call to return to Earth.

*   *   *

Later that evening, after he had told Velvet he was being called away, Laguz looked into her eyes as they lay beside one another. He tried to imprint the feeling of her skin, the look in her eyes and the smell of her hair into his soul; so that when she arrived on Earth he would know her, completely and instantly. Despite his anxiety and fear of losing her again, he knew that he would not give up the idea of living his life with her.

"What are you thinking?" she whispered.

He stroked her hair slowly and tried to smile. "I was thinking of how grateful I am you called for me. That we had this time together."

She nodded but didn't respond. A tear escaped down her cheek and he kissed it away. She was so beautiful. He had never known another soul to be so wise, so kind and so magickal. All he wanted, more than anything else in the whole Universe, was to stay right there, on the Other Side, with his arms around her, under the purple covers, in her bed. And he didn't need to be able to read her thoughts to know that she felt the same way.

He heard the call again and he closed his eyes and bowed his head.

Velvet sensed the shift in his energy and she tightened her grip on him. "Is it time?"

"Yes, it is."

*   *   *

"Hello, Starlight. What can I do for you?"

Starlight opened her eyes and smiled at Gold. "Gold, my dear, dear friend, I was just thinking about you, and I felt I should visit. How are you?"

Gold nodded, but Starlight noticed that his eye was twitching. A sure sign that he felt a little under pressure. "Good, good. Just trying to keep up with all these new changes. Who'd have thought it, eh? The Children arriving, the Academy ending, the world in such turmoil."

Starlight smiled. "Of course, I have Seen it all coming, and have Seen all that will transpire, so it is of no surprise to me."

"Well of course, I should have known you were behind it all." He winked to show that he was joking. He walked through the mist towards her, and held a hand out, which she took. "Could you let me See?"

"Are you sure? It will be difficult to watch, as I know you are quite fond of those who will be prominent figures in the fate of the Earth."

"I am sure. I hate being out of the loop as much as Velvet does. Show me."

"Very well." Starlight waved her hand through the mist, and a large, very wide screen appeared in front of them. Images began to scroll across the screen, streaming too fast for the human eye to comprehend, but then Gold was not human. He watched in horror at some parts, in happiness at others, but when the images came to an end, his horrified face turned to Starlight and he dropped her hand.

"That cannot be the end?" he whispered. "Are you certain?"

Starlight bit her lip. She had kept a portion of it to herself, because though she did not doubt her abilities, the last bit kept flickering, which meant that it was not set in stone.

"I'm afraid so, Gold." She sighed. "Now can you see my reluctance to show you? To know that the future holds an outcome that is not favourable, taints your actions from that point on."

"Is there any way to change it? I mean, we are talking about the actions of a few people here, surely we can influence their decisions?"

Starlight shook her head. "You would be amazed how difficult that is at times. And also how wrong it feels when you try. Ultimately, when you took the decision to grant them free will all those thousands of years ago, you released your power to just 'influence' them a little."

"I know. I'm still not sure that was the best decision I ever made. I mean, look at the mess on Earth! I know I created them so that I could experience everything, the good and the bad, but it amazes me just how crazy things have become."

Starlight squeezed his hand gently and released it. "It was the best decision you have ever made, Gold. They deserve to have the power over their own lives. They deserve such liberation. Those souls gave up their freedom to be constricted in a human body, to be weighed down by the dense vibrational energy. The least they deserve is to be able to decide their own fate."

Gold frowned and looked up at Starlight. "But that's the thing, I may have given them free will, but you have not, you still control their destiny, do you not? Why don't you change what is going to happen?"

Starlight sighed. "I already have. Believe me, out of all the possible outcomes I have foreseen, the one I have shown you is the best of them all."

"Goodness, if that's the best one, I'd hate to think what the others involved."

Starlight put her hand on Gold's shoulder. "Do not worry or fear what is to come, just continue to do as you are."

"Thank you, Starlight, I am doing my best. Though according to your insight, nothing I do will make much of a difference at this stage."

"Actually, Gold, what you do has a great significance in the outcome. Do not think that because of free will you cannot help. Because you can. You just have to wait for those who need help to ask for it, that's all."

Gold sighed. "Patience, I know. It's a virtue that I am running a little short of recently."

Starlight chuckled. "I must go, my friend. And I know that you have a meeting to attend, so I will keep you no longer."

"A meeting?" Gold frowned then suddenly remembered. "Oh, yes. The Elders. They wanted to discuss something with me about time or some such thing."

"Yes, please don't miss it, it will be integral to the changes that are about to take place."

"Of course, I never miss the Elder meetings." Gold's eye twitched and she hid a smile.

"Gold, it was lovely to catch up with you. I am sorry that I did not bring better visions of the future. Please understand though, that it is all perfect."

Gold smiled, but it didn't quite reach his eyes. "That's my line. Thank you, Starlight, I look forward to seeing you again. And please, let me know if anything changes."

Starlight nodded, wondering again about her decision to keep part of it to herself. For now, it seemed like the best thing to do. "Goodbye, Gold. Until we meet again."

"Yes, until then."

*   *   *

"Greetings, Laguz."

Laguz looked up at the Angel who stood in the mists before him and nodded. His heart was too full of grief to respond.

"I understand that you do not want to leave yet, that your time with Velvet has been too brief, but I can assure you, we do not mean to keep the two of you apart for very long."

"So Velvet will be coming to Earth soon?" Laguz's spirits lifted, he couldn't bear to spend another lifetime without his Flame.

"No. Velvet must wait until all of the Earth Angels in her care have left for Earth before she can leave too. But you will return to the Academy before she does. She will have a vision of you both together on Earth, so she'll know that you will go back to Earth together, at the same time, and be the same age."

Laguz's eyebrows lifted. "So this will only be a short lifetime, the one I am about to enter?"

"Relatively short, yes. But despite the brevity, it is very important."

Laguz nodded. "I understand. I wish I could have remained here longer, but if I get to be with Velvet soon, then I had better go."

"We are just waiting for someone."

Laguz frowned. "Who? Gold?"

The Angel shook her head. "No, we are waiting for the soul who will be your twin sister on Earth in this next lifetime."

"Oh, I see. I don't think I've ever been a twin before. Who is the soul, do I know them?"

"Hello, Laguz."

Laguz turned towards the familiar voice and saw Magenta approaching them. He held his arms out to her and they embraced. "Magenta. I didn't know you were here."

Magenta squeezed him gently then released him. "I was hidden away." Her expression became serious. "I just saw Velvet."

"Really? Is she okay?"

Magenta shook her head slightly. "No. But she will be. She is strong, you know that. She can pull through anything. She has come through much worse before."

Laguz's shoulders slumped. "Are you sure?" He looked over at the Angel who was waiting patiently. "Are you sure there is no way I can stay?"

The Angel shook her head with a soft smile on her lips. "This is the way is must be, Laguz. It will all work out, you'll see."

Laguz sighed. "It seems it is time for us to go then." He held out his hand to Magenta. "Are you ready, Sister?"

Magenta smiled and took his hand. "Yes, Brother, I am."

They turned to face the Angel and both closed their eyes, ready to begin their journey together.

Chapter Ten

"I heard that Velvet's Twin Flame was called yesterday, and that he left last night. Can you imagine, losing your Flame after just a few days? It must be horrible."

Corduroy had been ignoring his class up until that moment, but now he became still and listened hard to the chatter of his trainees as they completed their assignment on the ways a human could kill themselves.

"That's awful," a former Angel called Seraphinite said. "She must be in great pain right now. I hope she is being cared for."

"I still don't understand the concept of Twin Flames," a Starperson called Sphere said. "It is not something that we have on our planet. We do not attach ourselves to one particular being. We are all connected and all part of each other."

As they began a discussion on Twin Flames and what it was like to find the other half of your soul, Corduroy tuned out the conversation and tried to contain his joy. Laguz was gone. He had been called to Earth. Which meant that the chances of Laguz and Velvet being together were quite slim. A smile tugged at the corner of his mouth, and he struggled not to start jumping up and down. Velvet would be his now; he was sure of it. He just needed to tell her how he felt. After all, how strong could her bond with Laguz be if he was able to leave her so quickly and so easily? If he had really wanted to stay and be with her, he could have. He was clearly as weak as Corduroy had suspected all along.

Corduroy's foot tapped out the remaining minutes of his morning class, and as soon as it ended and the last trainee had been ushered out, he straightened his robes and clicked his fingers, reappearing outside Velvet's office. He didn't want to appear too eager, but then he also really wanted to be the one to take care of her in her time of need. Despite his dislike for Laguz, he knew that his absence would be causing Velvet pain, and he did not wish that upon her.

He started to knock, but the door vanished and a Faerie came zooming out. He stepped back out of sight, and she flew down the hall, oblivious to him. He watched her go and wondered if rushing in there was such a good idea after all. After a few minutes of debating with himself, he decided to wait. He had made it to the entrance of the gardens before changing his mind again and marching back up the hallway. He entered the office before he could think it through further, and the scene he was met with suddenly ignited the rage that he had been suppressing since Laguz had arrived at the Academy.

"What the hell is going on here?"

*   *   *

Linen sat on a bench in the Angelic Garden, feeling a little bit shaken still. After having a very successful meeting with a young Faerie called Aria, who had decided not to go to Earth, but to stay in the Fifth Dimension to teach at his new School; he had then had quite a shock.

Velvet had arrived back in the office, looking older and more haggard than she had ever looked before. Her hair was white again, and her purple robes were covered in sand. He had asked the Faerie to leave, feeling that Velvet would not want anyone to see her in such a state. He spoke to Velvet but got no response. He had tried to play some soothing music but the sound of the piano had caused her to erupt into sobs.

When he was trying to comfort her, Corduroy came in, and accused them of being up to no good. Linen shook his head to himself. As if Velvet would ever see him as anything other than her annoying assistant! It was quite preposterous. He wondered what Corduroy's problem was. From what Corduroy had said to Velvet, it sounded as though Laguz had left. He must have been called to Earth already. No wonder Velvet had been in such a state.

Linen sighed. Just when he thought things couldn't get any more complicated, the rules had changed again.

A flash of green caught his eye, and he looked up to see a dragonfly zoom past him. It reminded him of the Faerie, Aria. What an interesting soul she was. So bright and enthusiastic, so full of life. She was so happy that she was keeping her wings, that she seemed willing to do anything to help Linen. So Starlight had answered his prayer after all. She had sent him some help; he shouldn't have doubted that she would.

He tried to relax, and watched the waterfall for a while. It reminded him of his determination to go with the flow more. It was harder than he thought it might be. Because going with the flow meant surrendering to the fact that he really had no control over anything. He was just a log being carried along by the river, with no clue where he would wash up, or what he would bump into along the way.

A few souls walked by, and their loud voices in the quiet space made him jump. He hoped that he wouldn't bump into the Professor of Death again anytime soon.

*   *   *

They were making their way back to their room when it happened the first time.

"Yes, Mica?" Emerald asked, upon hearing her name.

"Yes, what? I didn't say anything," Mica replied.

Emerald halted suddenly in the middle of the corridor, bringing Mica to a sudden stop through their joined hands. She turned to him. "Did you hear anything?"

Mica shook his head. "No, I didn't. What did you hear?"

Emerald looked up and down the hallway, but it was deserted. "I heard them calling me. The Angels," she whispered.

Mica's eyes widened as he understood the meaning of her words. "To Earth?"

Emerald nodded and her grip on his hand tightened. "Why are they calling me and not you?"

"I don't know, maybe I will hear it too. Let's go back to the room for a while to rest."

Emerald heard the call a second time, this time it was louder and unmistakeable. "I won't be able to ignore it for very long. It will soon get louder."

"I know. But until then, let's just be together." Mica led her down the hallway to their room, and when inside, led her to the bed. They lay down beside each other and held each other close. Mica tried to think of something positive to say, something comforting and uplifting, but all he could think was - please don't leave me. His grip tightened and he breathed in her scent.

"I will find you," he whispered into her hair. "I promise you that I will find you."

*　　　*　　　*

Corduroy was so immersed in his anger, as he once again paced up and down his office, that he heard the voice several times before he paused to really listen and understand its significance. When he realised, he didn't know whether to feel happy or sad about it. In fact, other than his blinding rage, he really didn't feel much of anything at all.

His temper began to boil when he thought of the red-haired freak with his skinny little arms around Velvet, supposedly trying to comfort her. And when he thought about the fact that she had defended him, he become even more enraged. Linen had no right. He had barely been at the Academy for five minutes, he should not have been the one to comfort Velvet when she was suffering.

His thoughts swirled and stormed, and in the midst of it all, the Angelic voice continued to call his name, becoming louder and louder, bringing light into the darkness that he tried to cling to.

But it finally got to the point where he could ignore it no longer. He clicked his fingers and reappeared next to the bench in the Atlantis Garden.

For some reason, being there, staring at the gaping space where the stature of Laguz had once stood, Corduroy's darkness dissolved, leaving behind overwhelming sadness and regret.

When the call became louder still, he decided that it was now or never.

"Velvet, Velvet, Velvet. When you are free, please come to meet me in Atlantis."

*   *   *

Mica was completely unaware of Velvet's presence until he heard her whisper.

"Oh, Angel."

From his position on the floor, he couldn't see her face, but could hear the depth of her compassion, sympathy and shared pain in her ancient voice.

Eyes still closed, he tried to swallow the lump in his throat, but it wouldn't budge. He could still see Emerald's anguished expression as she had answered the call. The tears flowed freely down his face, soaking his silvery black robes. He felt Velvet's hand on his shoulder, and sensed her kneel on the floor next to him.

"I know that no words can bring you comfort in this moment. But I understand where you are right now, and I just want you to know that you are not alone. You are loved." Mica heard her voice falter. "And I am sure you will meet your Flame again."

Mica couldn't bring himself to speak, instead he leaned forwards into her velvety shoulder and she pulled him to her. They clung to each other for a few moments, like lone survivors, shipwrecked on an island.

"Thank you, Velvet," he managed to whisper.

She nodded into his shoulder, and after a few moments, he found the strength to pull away a little. Still holding each other's arms, they rose as one. Once he was sure that he was steady on his own feet, he let her go. He felt her hand on his face, and he finally looked up into her wise eyes. She had tears streaming down her cheeks, her pain a mirror of his own.

"We must remain strong, and keep going. The fate of the human world is in our hands."

Mica nodded, and took a deep breath. "I will do my best."

Velvet's hand dropped to her side and she tried to smile. "As will I." She sighed. "I must go, Angel. I am being called away. But if you need anything at all, please do come find me. Do not suffer this pain by yourself. I am here for you."

"Thank you, but I'm sure I will be okay," he reached out and touched her arm. "Please do not let me keep you any longer."

Velvet shook her head. "I just wish I could be of more help and comfort."

Mica tried to smile but failed. "Just knowing that you understand, is comfort enough."

"I must go." Velvet stepped forwards to hug Mica again. "Peace, love and light be with you always."

"And with you."

*   *   *

"Corduroy. My dear Old Soul."

"Hello, Angel," Corduroy muttered. He stared at the mist at their feet and tried to blink back the tears that were threatening to fall. He felt his Guardian Angel's hand on his shoulder and then her other hand lifted his head. He met her eyes, and the tears fell freely.

"Corduroy, I know that you are in pain, and that you try to hide it, but there is no need. I am your Guardian Angel. I am a part of you. I am here to guide you, love you and protect you. You need not hide your feelings from me, for they are my feelings also."

Corduroy wiped his eyes with the sleeve of his robes. "I know, Angel. It is a habit. I do my best not to show the real me. No one wants to see that."

"Now I know you do not believe that."

"You saw how Velvet reacted just now when I let down my barriers and confessed my love for her. She was repulsed." Corduroy swallowed hard. Just thinking of her moving away from him, of her rejection, caused him more pain than he thought was possible to bear.

"She was not repulsed, she was surprised. You should know that throughout your many lifetimes together, she has never known the depth of your feelings. Which is precisely why you might like to use this next life on Earth to begin being more open and honest about your feelings. They are no good locked away."

"Is that my mission for this lifetime? To become a sappy, feminine man who cries all the time and talks about his feelings? Or perhaps I'll be gay or a woman, so I can properly express my feminine side." Corduroy knew that speaking to his Guardian Angel in this sarcastic way was uncalled for and spiteful, but he didn't care. She would love him unconditionally anyway. She was probably the only being in the Universe who ever had or ever would.

"You will be a male, and your mission will be of your own choosing."

Corduroy frowned. "You mean you aren't going to help me decide? You've never let me choose before."

"Of course, your general mission is to help with the Awakening, which is why all Earth Angels are going to Earth right now. But your personal mission is up to you. You can choose to remain the way you are, and live a human life filled with rage, hate and bitterness; or you can transform those feelings and live a life of joy. It is your choice."

"How kind of you." Corduroy sighed. He couldn't seem to stop the nasty words from spewing from his mouth. But he was angry, sad, and rejected. He couldn't fathom a life of joy and happiness at this point.

"Are you ready?" his Angel asked softly. "Your family are waiting for you."

Corduroy nodded. He dared not to speak for fear of saying something else he would regret.

"I shall see you again, but until then, I am but a thought, a whisper, or a wish away."

Corduroy nodded again, and this time did nothing to stem the tears that slid down his cheeks. He felt the squeeze of the Angel's hand briefly on his shoulder before the misty world melted away, and his new life began.

Chapter Eleven

Indigo Batik sat in his office after the day's classes and stared at the artwork on his wall. Ever since he had visited the Golden City, he had not been able to concentrate. It had been indescribably wonderful, seeing his siblings again and spending time in the city. The feeling of being home again was so overwhelming that a tear slid down his cheek.

He did not regret leaving the Indigo World so long ago. And he did not regret a single moment he had spent in service at the Academy. But he felt as though his time was done. He wanted to go home. He wiped the tear away. He would go and see Velvet. He was sure that she would understand.

He stood and clicked his fingers, appearing outside Velvet's office. He knocked and the door disappeared.

"Good evening, Linen."

Linen looked up and smiled. "Professor Indigo. You just caught me, I just popped back to get something. I meant to come and see you earlier, to see how things went with the Indigo Child."

"I have come here tonight hoping to talk with Velvet about it, actually."

"I'm afraid Velvet just left, but if you knock on her door, she may still be awake."

"I don't wish to disturb her, but it is quite important."

"In that case I am sure she will not mind."

"Thank you, Linen." Indigo turned back towards the door, then stopped. "And thank you for bringing the Child to me. I appreciate it."

Linen shrugged. "You're welcome. Have a good night."

Indigo nodded and left the office. He walked down the hallway until he reached Velvet's purple door. He hesitated before knocking; he hated to disturb her out of hours, but he felt that if he delayed his request, he may get called to Earth and it would be too late to change course.

He tapped lightly on the door, and seconds later, the door disappeared and Velvet was stood there in a thin robe, looking surprised and very tired.

"Indigo, I wasn't expecting you, is everything okay?"

Indigo nodded, but then shook his head. "I'm so sorry to come to your room like this, but I feared that if I left it until morning it may be too late."

Velvet frowned, but ushered him inside. "Please, have a seat." She gestured to the purple velvet-covered chair next to her bed. He sat down, and she clicked her fingers, so that she was now dressed in her day robes.

"I know that you are aware of my origins, and that a long time ago I came from the Golden City in the Indigo World."

Velvet nodded and sat on the edge of her bed. "Yes, I knew that."

"I thought that I would never be able to return home, and so I never wished to talk about it." Indigo looked up at Velvet, a tear slid down his cheek. "But then the Children arrived here, and one of them came to visit me. She took me to the part of the city they travelled here with, and I transformed into my true form again." A smile broke out across his face. "It was amazing, Velvet, I was truly myself again." He sighed. "And so, though it pains me to let you down in any way, after working for you for so many years; I have decided that I do not wish to return to Earth." More tears slid down his cheeks. "I wish to return home."

Velvet also had tears in her eyes when she stood up and held her arms open to the professor. He stood, and she hugged him. "Of course you should go home, my friend," she whispered in his ear. "You have free will, you may do as you wish. But never, for one moment, believe that you are letting me down. You have given everything to this Academy, and I can ask no more of you than that. Go home, Indigo Child. Go home."

Indigo nodded into her shoulder. "Thank you, Velvet. It has been a pleasure working for you all these years. You are the wisest and most beautiful soul I have ever met."

Velvet squeezed him tight then released him. She stepped back and smiled. "Thank you. Goodbye, Indigo. Have a safe journey home."

Indigo nodded. "I will. Goodbye, Velvet." He smiled at her once more, before leaving. Outside Velvet's door, he could not wait a second longer. He clicked his fingers and reappeared outside room 333.

He walked into the room and was immediately surrounded by his siblings. Joyfully he turned back into a blue sphere of light and zoomed back to the Golden City with them all. He excitedly communicated his good news.

Within moments, they had sent him on his way, and he travelled through space and time, through the stars and galaxies, finally going home to where he belonged.

*   *   *

Linen felt exhausted yet unable to close his eyes. The events of the day ran through his mind, and it felt impossible that so much had happened in such a short space of time. At least he had managed to see Aria again. He wanted to make sure that she wouldn't tell everyone about the state Velvet had been in.

Linen smiled at the thought of Aria. She was so sweet. He was looking forward to working with her.

He thought of Velvet and his smile turned into a frown. He really hoped she would be okay. He had found her in the office earlier, playing the piano. She had only just rediscovered her ability to play. He had watched her for a while, and the music had haunted him. He knew that the Flames were being reunited on Earth in the next few years, and part of him wondered if that truly was the best thing for all. If it was difficult in this dimension to lose a Twin Flame, even though both parties knew without a doubt that they would one day meet again, how hard would it be to lose a Twin Flame on Earth? Without the certainty of knowing they would meet again? Surely it would destroy the one left behind?

Linen sighed. He really should be putting in extra hours to get the School ready to operate. Things were moving so quickly that even the professors were now being called to Earth. Not that Linen minded that Corduroy had now gone. It meant he didn't have to constantly look over his shoulder anymore. And Indigo. He wondered if he had been called too. He seemed fairly desperate to see Velvet, perhaps it was because he wanted to say goodbye before he left?

Linen closed his eyes and tried to relax. He wanted to be fresh and awake for his meeting with Aria in the morning. He smiled at the thought of seeing the Faerie again. He was going to enjoy working with her, he could just tell.

"Thank you, Starlight, thank you."

* * *

From her home among the stars, Starlight smiled as she watched the latest events. She was pleased for Indigo, and watched his progress through the Universe as he returned home. He deserved to go back after all he had given Earth and the Academy. She was also pleased that Linen was feeling a little less overwhelmed now he had Aria's help. Of course, the fact that they were Twin Flames really was just the finishing touch of perfection. She would enjoy watching the two of them discover that. She watched them meet in the office in the morning, and saw Velvet send them to the Elemental Realm, to begin their recruitment for teachers for the new School. Linen had proved himself far beyond what she had hoped for when she had asked him to take on the mission. She couldn't help but be a little proud of the young Faerie boy who was about to change the world.

*   *   *

"You have wings! Linen! That's so awesome!"

Linen hovered above the ground, a huge grin on his face. "Wow! It feels so amazing to fly again." He did a few circles around Aria and she giggled.

"Can you see why I didn't want to give them up now?"

"Absolutely. This feels so great!" Linen looked around them, then looked down at his case, which had shrunk in size too. "Perhaps this is just what happens when you visit the Elemental Realm. I might not get to keep them."

Aria frowned. "That sucks. Oh well, I guess you should just enjoy them while you have them."

Linen smiled. "That's a very good point, and I will! Thank you, Aria."

Aria shrugged her tiny shoulders. "You're welcome. Now then, what do we do first?"

"Well, I spoke to the recruitment Faeries, and they told me that there's a Faerie Hub of sorts, in a giant toadstool, where they post notices. And one of them posted the call for teachers for me yesterday. They assured me that news travels fast here, so there should be some responses by now."

"Oh yes, Faeries love to talk, didn't you know that?"

Linen laughed. "Oh, really? I hadn't noticed." He flew ahead, and Aria followed him. They reached a large fallen branch and Linen nodded. "Yes we are nearly there, just a few more moments and we should see it."

When they went around a large tree trunk they stopped suddenly at the sight of the giant toadstool.

"Wow," Aria gasped. "That's so cool! I don't think I ever saw this part of the Elemental Realm when I was here."

"It is quite impressive," Linen agreed. They flew to the front door at the base of the toadstool and entered. Inside, there was a spiral staircase in the centre, and curved walls full of noticeboards. Most of them were notices of land that was about to be destroyed. Aria flew around them, reading the warnings. Her earlier happy mood evaporated.

"All of these Faeries will be out of work now, just as I was when they destroyed my grass patch," she said sadly.

Linen flew to her and put his hand on her shoulder. He felt a little tingle when his skin touched hers. "That's why we are here, Aria, to give them a new purpose."

Aria nodded and looked up at him. Linen wondered if she felt the sparks too. She flew to the other side of the circular room and her face lit up. "Here it is! Here's our poster! And look! The sign-up sheet for interviews is full!"

Linen smiled at all of the exclamations and flew over to join her. He looked at all of the tiny handprints covering the list and raised an eyebrow. "We will have to give them individual names when they join the School. For now we will have to assign them numbers to distinguish between them. I guess we'd better get started, the recruitment Faeries said they would arrange an interview room for us, upstairs. We'd better go up and prepare, the first on the list will probably be arriving soon."

"Oh, this is so exciting!" She flew to the stairs and looked at them, frowning. "Why on Earth do they have stairs when we can all fly?"

"For those of us who can't," an ant, who was making his way up the spiral staircase, replied.

"Oh!" Aria said. "Of course, I am so sorry." She looked

up at Linen who was taking down the sign-up sheet from the wall. "I wonder if Larry is still okay, it would be lovely to see him."

"Larry?"

"He was my best friend. He's a ladybug."

"Well, if we get done here early enough, would you like to try and find him?"

Aria flew into Linen's arms and squeezed him hard. "Oh, that would be so amazing! Yes, please!"

Linen chuckled. "Let's get started then."

Aria looked up the staircase, then looked back at Linen. "Wanna race?"

*   *   *

When he had heard that former Earth Angels were returning to Earth to help with the spiritual Awakening that was apparently in the process of happening; Cobalt knew immediately that he should also return.

Despite his last experience on Earth fulfilling all of his personal needs, he knew that if there was a chance of the Golden Age happening, he wanted to be there to experience it.

He'd also heard whispers of the Flames being reunited, but that wasn't a huge motivation for returning, because he had never met his Twin Flame. He was an Angel, but he had lived many lives on Earth as a human. Too many, he truly felt. But not once, in any of those lives, had he met the one. His other half. His Flame.

So he wasn't going back to Earth for himself, and it was not in the hope of finally meeting his Flame. He felt deeply that it was important to go, because he was an Angel, and helping people was what he was created to do.

He arrived in the foyer of the Earth Angel Training Academy, and read the information on the board there. Apparently, all he had to do was state his name and origin, and he would be assigned a room.

"Cobalt, Angelic Realm," he said. His palm tingled and he looked down to see a number appear in purple glitter on it. He looked back at the noticeboard to see a map of the Academy. He found where his room was, but because his sense of direction wasn't the best, he didn't hold much hope of finding his way there without getting lost at least once.

He set off down the corridor, smiling and nodding at anyone he passed. He kept picturing the map in his mind, but by the time he'd made two turns, he was already lost.

Cobalt was stood in the hallway, wondering whether to continue the way he was going, or to retrace his steps and begin again, when someone bumped into him.

"Oh! I'm so sorry, I wasn't paying attention."

He turned around to see the most beautiful soul he had seen in a long time. He smiled at her. In that instant, he knew he was in the right place.

*   *   *

At the end of the last interview, Aria and Linen went through the list and decided which Faeries they would like to interview again, as they only had so many slots and couldn't hire all of their favourites. They would also have to visit other parts of the Realm to interview Faeries, as it was only fair.

"Can we go and find Larry now?" Aria asked, bouncing up and down in excitement.

Linen smiled and put all of his paperwork back into his case. "I don't see why not, I'm sure we won't be missed at the Academy right now. Where will we find him?"

"Hmm, that's a good question. I was so excited when I left the Elemental Realm for the Academy that I didn't notice where everyone else was moving on to. We could try near to where I lived, I guess."

"Okay, lead the way."

Aria and Linen left the toadstool, posting the list of Faeries who would be interviewed again on the wall on their way out. Aria flew over to a little sign just outside.

"Awesome! They still run the service! We should be able to catch a ride from here. It's quite far, you see, we'd get tired if we tried to fly."

Linen frowned. "My memories of being a Faerie are pretty hazy now, what service is that?"

"The Sparrow Express. They're pretty regular, one should be along soon." Aria looked up. "Oh look, here's one now!" She waved her arms enthusiastically at the bird flying towards them. It dove down then hovered next to them.

"Where can I take you two?" the sparrow asked.

Aria flew over to it and sat on its back, holding onto its feathers. Linen followed her and sat behind her.

"To the Crazy Oak Tree, please!"

"As you wish." With that, the sparrow shot upwards and Linen grabbed onto Aria, afraid he was about to fall off. Aria giggled and yelled out.

"Wooo! This is so much fun! I should have done this more when I lived here!"

Linen clutched her tighter as they rose higher up into the air. Soon, they were so high that Linen could see human houses, roads and people. He found it amazing that there was an entire world hidden within the human world that most humans didn't believe existed. If only they knew! If only they believed in magick.

He thought of the Faeries that he used to talk to in his own garden. Some people knew. Some still believed. He just hoped that the Earth Angels and the Children would be able to convince more humans to believe too.

Sure that he wasn't in danger of falling, Linen relaxed a little and began to enjoy the breeze whipping past his face and fluttering through his wings.

All too soon, they started their descent, and the sparrow

landed on a low branch in an oak tree, next to another little Sparrow Express sign. There were two Faeries waiting there for a ride. Linen and Aria dismounted the sparrow, and the two other Faeries hopped on.

"Thank you, Mr Sparrow! Have a great day."

The sparrow nodded to Aria then flew off. Aria turned to Linen, her cheeks red and her green eyes wide. "Wasn't that amazing? It's so much fun here in the Elemental Realm. Perhaps we should just stay here, and not go back to the Academy."

Linen knew that she was mostly kidding, but he was struck with a sudden longing to do just that. To shrug off the responsibility that he had been burdened with and just be a Faerie again. He could live here, flying on sparrows and living simply and joyfully. With Aria. He looked into her eyes and smiled. "That does sound good."

Aria frowned. "I was only joking, we couldn't stay here, what about the Children? They need us!" She flew down through the branches to the base of the tree and after a moment, Linen followed her. She was right, of course, but for a moment, contemplating such joyful freedom had made his spirit soar.

*   *   *

"So have you Seen anything good recently?"

Leon looked up from his notebook to see Cerise enter the room. He felt a little annoyed, he had hoped to be alone for a while to make sense of all the connections between himself, Velvet and Laguz. "It would be difficult to know where to begin, to be honest. I thought that perhaps I would have trouble Seeing while in this human body, but the visions have become clearer and stronger than ever before."

Cerise smiled. "So you're getting used to the body then? I've never known any different, personally. I've never had to go through what you have. I've just been a regular human since the beginning of my existence." She went to her bed and sat down, propping herself up against the mountain of pillows.

"I very much doubt that you have ever been just a regular human," Leon commented. "If that were so, you would not be here, and you would not be passionate about learning how to help the world."

Cerise shrugged. "I suppose you are right. I just get a little gloomy sometimes. Do you honestly think we can make a difference? That we could actually guide the world into the first-ever Golden Age?"

"Are you asking me for my opinion, or are you asking me if I have Seen it?"

Cerise smiled. "Though I'm sure your opinion would be a good one, I was wondering if you had Seen it, actually."

Leon looked down at his notebook, which Professor Chiffon had very kindly magickally enlarged for him. "It's difficult to say," he paused and looked up at Cerise, who nodded for him to continue. "I have had visions of myself on Earth. I have Seen some of my life and my path, and I have also Seen myself interacting with other Earth Angels from the Academy when we are human on Earth." He didn't mention that those Earth Angels were the current Head of the Academy and her Flame.

"That's really cool. Do we meet on Earth?"

"I haven't Seen you in my Earth future yet, but perhaps we will. After all, isn't that part of the reason why we are meeting now? So that we might recognise each other as humans?"

"Yes, I believe it is." Cerise settled back and closed her eyes. "I think I might get a little rest before my next class."

"Of course." Leon closed his notebook and tucked it into his pocket. "I think I might go for a walk. Get some fresh air before spending another hour talking about death."

Cerise smiled sadly, her eyes still closed. "I miss Professor Corduroy's classes, if I'm honest. He was pretty intense."

Leon raised an eyebrow, even though Cerise couldn't see him. "Intense is a polite way of putting it."

"I think he must have been quite sensitive and sweet really, and that the Professor of Death persona was just a mask."

Leon paused on his way to the door and blinked as a vision appeared before him of Cerise on Earth. She was walking along, hand in hand with... Corduroy? Leon blinked several more times, and the vision flickered away. "Maybe you're right," he replied softly.

"I know I'm right," Cerise said, as he left the room.

*   *   *

Starlight sighed happily. It was all working in perfect synchronicity, exactly as she had foreseen. Better, in fact. She had loved watching Linen and Aria in the Elemental Realm, the joy on Aria's face when she had been reunited with Larry was just priceless. As was the look on Linen's face when they had encountered some Leprechauns and he thought that Aria was going to invite them to be teachers at the new School.

Starlight laughed to herself. That certainly would have thrown everything off. The Leprechauns, though highly intelligent and amusing, were far too mischievous to be teachers at the School. She remembered fondly the time they had caused havoc at the Academy. Velvet had almost had a breakdown at that time, and came very close to quitting.

Starlight shook her head. That would also have thrown the Universal plan way off. Velvet was so important to the fate of the Universe, and yet she really had no idea. She thought that she was just an Old Soul. Just the Head of the Academy, but she was so, so much more than that. And one day, when the time was right, Starlight would be able to show her that.

One day, Starlight would have the pleasure of welcoming her sister home again.

Chapter Twelve

Cobalt spent the afternoon in the Angelic Garden, feeling quite at home on the golden bench in front of the waterfall. He couldn't believe that within ten minutes of arriving at the Academy, he had met her. His Twin Flame. He was as certain that she was the one as he was of his own name.

He closed his eyes and pictured her beautiful face, her soft blonde hair and her Angelic smile. Amethyst. Such a perfect name for such a wonderful soul.

He wondered then why they couldn't have met before in the Angelic Realm. It bothered him that now he was at the Academy, he could be called to Earth at any moment. Though they had only just met, and had spent less than a couple of hours together, he knew that being separated from her would cause him pain.

He wished he could see more of her today, but she had classes all afternoon, and he had an evening session to attend. Although there was a bit of time in-between their sessions.

Without giving it another thought, he hopped up off of the bench and headed back to the Academy. She had told him which room she was in, perhaps they could spend a little time together, if she was free.

He walked quickly in what he thought was the right direction, hoping to catch his Angel.

*　　*　　*

Gold found it difficult to concentrate on his duties after his meeting with the Elders. He knew that he could not put off telling Velvet the news much longer. She needed to know of the recent developments as they were very important to the way she was running the Academy. But he knew what the information would mean to her, ultimately. And it had nothing to do with the class schedules of the trainees. He paced up and down, the mist swirling around the bottom of his heavy robes.

He became aware of a soul approaching. The soul had left Earth in an accident. Gold stopped pacing and straightened up, then turned to greet the soul, who was human.

"Where am I?" The soul looked around him wearily. "I'm dead, aren't I?"

Gold nodded slowly. It was interesting to see that human souls were coming to this awareness more quickly than ever before. He remembered times not many Earthly years ago where it would take some time to convince souls of their demise, and get them to understand.

"You are indeed on the Other Side," Gold said, stepping towards him. "And I must ask you a very important question."

The soul frowned. "What is it?"

"Do you want to stay?"

The frown turned into a look of surprise. "You mean I can choose whether or not I stay?"

"Indeed. It was not technically your time to pass over here, and if you so wished, you could return. Or, if you prefer, you can move on to the Angelic Realm, where you can rest until you decide on the next part of your soul's progression, with the guidance of your Guardian Angel."

"Wow. That's a lot of information to take in at once." The soul scratched his head, messing up his hair on one side. "How long do I have to decide?"

"A few minutes." Though it didn't really matter how long

it took him to decide, after all, time was an illusion, Gold found it was easier to give them a time limit to work to, otherwise they could ponder the question forever. And though Gold would welcome the delay, he knew he couldn't put off the inevitable for much longer.

"I want to stay. I know what happened was an accident, but to be honest I wasn't very happy, I don't think I want to go back to that life."

"Are you quite certain? Perhaps you could give your life a second chance? Turn things around?"

The soul shook his head. "No, I want to stay."

"Very well then." Gold stepped to the side and gestured to the gates off in the distance behind him. "Please proceed to the Angelic Realm. Pearl will be at the gates, she will help you find your Guardian."

The soul smiled. "Thank you." He held out his hand and Gold shook it, smiling back. He watched the soul walk through the mists towards the gates, and the smile slipped from his face.

He really could not delay any longer, it was time. With a sigh, he called for his replacement to come and take over for a while, then he clicked his fingers.

*　　　*　　　*

Aria's eyes were wide when they entered room 333. Though she had seen the city briefly when it had arrived, thanks to her snooping with her friend Amethyst, it was even more spectacular up close.

She was mesmerised by the blue spheres of light shooting around the Golden City, forming the most intricate patterns.

"Good afternoon, Indigo Children!" Linen called out. Almost immediately, the lights stopped moving and all zoomed towards them, turning into Children on the way. They lined up in perfect rows in front of Aria and Linen. Much to his disappointment, Linen had indeed returned to his Old Soul body upon returning to the Academy.

"Good afternoon, Linen. Who is your Faerie friend?" The tiny blonde Indigo Child asked.

"I'm Aria! I'm helping Linen with the new School."

"Lovely to meet you, Aria. I am sure he needs the help, it is a big task." She turned back to Linen, "How can we be of help to you today? Is it time for us to attend classes?"

Linen shook his head. "No, not yet, I'm afraid, we are still recruiting teachers right now."

"Be sure not to delay, I sense there are more changes afoot that will speed things along greatly, and we wish to be fully prepared before beginning our Earthly missions."

"We are working as quickly as we can. One of the reasons we are here now, as well as for you to meet Aria, is to find out what you know about the changes that are about to occur."

The blonde Indigo Child turned to her siblings and communicated silently with them. They nodded in unison, then transformed back into blue spheres of light and returned to the city. She turned back to Linen and Aria.

"I can answer your questions, though I am afraid I may not have as many answers as you may like. Until the visit from the Angel, we were blissfully unaware of the situation on Earth. And as you know, our connection with the Indigo Children who left for Earth long ago has been severed. So we cannot link directly with them for answers either." She smiled. "Though thanks to you, one of our lost brothers is now returning home. He has agreed to look after the Indigo World while I am on Earth."

Linen frowned. "Do you mean Professor Indigo? He has returned to your world?"

"Yes, he wanted to go home. He will be there soon. It takes a little while to get there."

"So it is possible to return home, even when you've been gone for a long time?" Linen asked, thinking of what Aria had said about staying in the Elemental Realm.

"Of course it is. Though sometimes it is necessary to release the past, including the people and memories in it, in order to return. Indigo may find that he will lose some of his memories of being on Earth and here at the Academy, though he will remember that he has done well, and that his new purpose is to look after our siblings still living there."

Linen looked at Aria. If returning to the Elemental Realm permanently meant losing her, then he wasn't willing to take the risk. Aria looked at him and frowned a little, as though she could hear his thoughts.

He turned back to the Child. "So what do you know of the timescale we are working with? It would just be useful to know what kind of teaching schedule we should be planning for the classes. Do we have days, weeks, or months? What are the most important lessons that you need to learn?"

The Indigo Child looked around the room, empty of anything other than the Golden City. "Shall we find somewhere more comfortable, perhaps? I will then tell you all that I know."

"We could go to the gardens," Aria said. "You might like the Planetary Garden, it's pretty cool there."

The Child smiled. "Sounds perfect."

*   *   *

"I'm sorry that I was unable to help you, Gold."

Gold looked up at Starlight. "You knew of the time changes?"

"Of course I knew," Starlight moved through the mist, her wings sparkling in the dim light. "It was my idea. Even though it hurt Velvet, something I am loathe to do, it was necessary."

Gold sighed. "I'm sure it must be, otherwise it would not be so. About Velvet though, are you sure I still cannot warn her of the bigger picture?"

"And cause her to lose faith entirely?" Starlight shook her head. "Oh, Gold, I know you wish nothing but the best for her, I do too, but telling her what her future holds is not the best thing for her. She must discover and experience it for herself. In some ways, I am sorry that I showed it to you," Starlight touched Gold's cheek softly. "You have a sadness in your eyes that you did not have before."

Gold looked into Starlight's bright eyes. "I just wish there was more that I could do, my friend. I feel as though I am not fulfilling my duties here."

"You are exactly where you should be, Gold. You are fulfilling your purpose perfectly."

"Thank you. Does it seem silly that I should lose faith in myself?"

"It seems perfectly natural. And know that in time, not only will you regain your faith in yourself, but millions of people on Earth will also find their faith in you once more. They will see you as you truly are, and you will help them to move forward and Awaken."

"I look forward to that."

"I must go, Gold." Starlight stepped forwards and embraced him. "I believe in you."

Gold stepped back and smiled. Starlight disappeared, leaving behind a few sparkling lights in the mist.

"Goodbye, Starlight."

*   *   *

When Mica heard Velvet's words, they were like an arrow to his heart. He had feared that he might never find Emerald on Earth, just being a few days or weeks behind, but now that the timescales had changed, he could be born on Earth years after her. He left the main hall, his vision blurry with his tears. He ignored the souls around him, and focussed on making it to the Angelic Garden, which was where he felt most connected to

Emerald. Without any effort or concentration, he found his way there and sat on their favourite bench, in front of the waterfall.

He was silently praying for the Angels to call him. Surely they wouldn't make the gap too big? He wished again that he had heeded his sense of foreboding and had insisted that he and Emerald stayed in the Angelic Realm. After all, it was the only place that they had ever managed to find one another. They had never had a human life together, even though between them, they'd had several human lives. They had been part of the very early waves of Earth Angels, those who had begun the changes on Earth long before humans on Earth were ready for them. They had lived difficult lives, as they were outcast, misunderstood and generally mistaken for being a bit crazy. In those lives they had each acutely felt the loss of their connection to one another. Each time they had met again in the Angelic Realm, Mica had sworn he would never let her go again.

But he had.

And now he faced another lifetime without her.

He didn't bother wiping away his tears, he let them fall freely, knowing that it didn't matter what others passing by thought of him. He closed his eyes and imagined her face. Her sparkling green eyes, her beautiful smile, and a sob escaped from him.

"Shhh, it's okay. You'll find her again. I know you will."

Mica felt a hand on his shoulder, and opened his eyes to find a very serious-looking soul with twinkly grey eyes and short grey hair sat next to him.

"How do you know?" Mica asked quietly, drying his cheeks with his sleeve.

"Because I am a Seer. I can See you together with your beloved, and I can See you both being instrumental in the Awakening of the humans on Earth. You are Twin Flames, aren't you?"

Mica nodded, his spirits lifting slightly.

"You will meet her, and you will know her instantly. She may not be in the position to reciprocate immediately, but you will be together quite quickly. Then you will work together to re-unite the Flames. It is your mission, and hers. And you will succeed."

For the first time since he had said goodbye to Emerald, Mica felt hope. "Thank you," he said, the tears in his eyes now ones of joy and love. "You have no idea how much that means to me to hear that. What is your name?"

"Leon. First-year trainee and former Faerie." Leon held his hand out but instead of shaking it, Mica pulled him into a hug.

He pulled back. "Mica, second-year trainee and former Angel. But I guess you already knew that, huh?"

Leon chuckled. "I only See that which I am supposed to. I don't make a habit of prying into the lives of others, but I could sense that you were in need of some hope."

"And you were right. I'm very glad you decided to tell me what you could See."

Leon nodded. "You are welcome. Now, please excuse me, I'm late for a class."

"Of course. I hope to see you again, Leon."

"I have no doubt that you will."

*　　*　　*

Cobalt walked back to his room after his meeting with Amethyst, with conflicting emotions. He was so incredibly happy, and clearly he looked it, considering all of the smiles he received on his way through the Academy. But he also felt an all-consuming emptiness the moment he had released her hand and walked away from her.

He shook his head at himself. The feelings were so strong and yet they seemed so irrational. He had never felt such a deep kinship and connection to another being before, in all of his existence. It unnerved him slightly.

He reached his room, without getting lost for once, and entered, intending to get some sleep. However, he found that his mind wouldn't calm down enough to let him rest. He lay on his bed and stared up at the high ceiling. His roommates were not there, and he could hear nothing but the sound of his own thoughts.

He closed his eyes and let his mind wander. Suddenly, a vision of the Angels calling him popped into his head. He thought about leaving Amethyst behind and his heart felt as though it had been wrenched from his chest.

His eyes flew open and he sat up, panting. He knew, logically, that the pain he felt in that moment was purely in his mind. Pain did not exist in this dimension. But he also knew that it was a preview of the pain he would feel if he were to lose Amethyst while they were on Earth. If they were even lucky enough to find each other.

Cobalt breathed deeply and calmed himself, before laying back down on the bed. He had watched humans on Earth for a long time before his own first human incarnation. He had seen them find their soulmates, lose their soulmates, and miss meeting their soulmates altogether. He had been an Angel of Connection and he had seen every emotion, every possibility, every joy and every pain.

But this was something different. This was the first time in this age that the Flames were being reunited, and their connection was deeper than any other possible connection. It was ancient, it was all-consuming, it was perfect, and the loss of it was pain beyond imagination.

Experiencing the connection first-hand meant that he understood why it was essential for the Flames to be reunited. He believed that if enough souls on Earth found their Twin Flames, then Earth would have no choice but to Awaken and move into the Golden Age.

*   *   *

"Gold?"

Gold turned towards the Angelic Realm from his usual post and peered into the mists. "Yes?"

An Angel flew towards him, hovering just a few feet away. She bowed her head to him. "I bring news of Velvet."

Gold sighed. With immeasurable speed, he remembered how badly Velvet had reacted to the time change from the vision that Starlight had shared with him. "Is she okay?"

"She has left her body in the Fifth Dimension, and her spirit is currently in the Angelic Realm. She seems calmer now, but I get the sense that she wishes not to return to the Academy."

Gold sighed again, he could feel his eye beginning to twitch. "Thank you for letting me know, Opalite. I think it best if we leave her be. After all, she has free will, we cannot force her to return."

Opalite frowned. "But Gold, the fate of the world is depending on her to-"

Gold held up his hand to interrupt. "I know, Opalite, I know. I have seen what will happen. I know the situation."

Opalite's cheeks reddened slightly. "Of course. My apologies for assuming you didn't."

Gold waved his hand dismissively. "Just ensure that she is not disturbed. She must have this time to reflect, and then she must decide for herself if she wishes to return."

Opalite nodded. "I assume that some may come looking for her?"

"Yes, I should think so. Perhaps you can warn Pearl for me."

"I will, Gold." She smiled and then flew back towards the gates.

Gold turned back to face the misty void and sighed. He

wished he could spare all those in his kingdom the pain that they felt, but he knew that it was a necessary part of life. It was why the human experience on Earth had been created. So that souls could experience everything. The good and the bad. The torture and exquisite joy. The pleasure and the sorrow.

And when they felt it, he felt it too.

He relived in his mind the fate of the world as Starlight had shown him, and he felt heavier. What he had seen happen was already happening. Therefore it seemed certain that no matter what happened from here on, his children would all be returning home to him soon.

Chapter Thirteen

Linen spent the evening in the office, making notes of everything the Indigo Child had told them. She was right, she didn't have as many answers as he would have liked, and Linen got the feeling that she knew more than she had shared with him.

One of the things that bothered him was that there weren't that many Children. He'd tried to do a quick count yesterday, and though he wasn't sure, he thought there were only about a hundred of them. How were one hundred Children going to make much of a difference on Earth? He had asked if there were any Indigo Children in any other Academies in the Fifth Dimension, but apparently there were not. There would be only one School for the Children. He had asked if more Children would be coming, and she had frowned for a moment before responding.

"There are no more Indigos coming here. We are the only ones," she had said.

Linen leaned back in his chair. What was the point? Even with hundreds of Earth Angels on Earth, it was doubtful whether the changes would be dramatic enough to make a difference. Linen tapped his pen on the desk. Surely this wasn't all that Starlight had planned?

He looked through the rest of his notes. The Indigo Child hadn't been sure of the timescale, but she was confident that things would move along a lot quicker than any of them had imagined.

He sighed. He would just have to be patient. He got up and decided to go and visit the recruitment office. He needed to arrange the interviews in the Angelic Realm and the second interviews in the Elemental Realm.

Perhaps things would start to become clear in the morning.

*   *   *

Starlight sighed in response to Linen's thoughts. The poor Faerie had no idea what was to come the following day. She had watched Velvet bring the lightning down upon herself in a fit of despair. Despite knowing it would happen, it still saddened Starlight to see Velvet in such pain. She wished she could whisper the words that would bring her comfort. But the pain was necessary. As all pain was necessary. Without it, how could joy possibly be known?

She was glad that Velvet had gone to the Angelic Realm, she would find peace and comfort there.

Starlight shook off her sadness. She knew that Velvet would be okay very soon, and that Linen would play his part in her revival. Besides, she had a very pleasant job ahead of her. The Crystal Children were nearly at the Academy; their arrival was imminent. She had arranged for a message to be delivered when they arrived. But it would not end there. Linen was right in his thoughts, one hundred Indigo Children was not enough. And there were only two hundred Crystal Children. For the world to truly experience the Golden Age, which despite the uncertain, flickering future, Starlight felt sure would happen, they would need more Children than that.

Starlight had not yet visited the Rainbow World. But she had seen its glittering beauty from afar. She was excited to finally be in the position where a visit was necessary. Unlike the Indigo and Crystal Children, the Rainbows had never before left their world for another. Starlight knew that there was a possibility that they may not get to Earth, but she had to ask them if they would be willing to go.

If they said no, she was sure that the future that flickered with uncertainty would flicker out completely, and only darkness would be left.

She closed her eyes, and then opened them again when she felt the beauty of the Rainbows wash over her. She smiled and an involuntary giggle escaped. She was in the most beautiful technicolour land, with rolling hills of orange grass, blue trees and a pink sky. Clear crystals hung from every branch, and sparkled from every surface. Every flower had a core of clear, faceted crystal. In the beaming sunlight, everywhere she looked, Rainbows danced. It was impossible not to feel happy and joyful in their presence. Following her intuition, she held out her hand and when a Rainbow landed in it, she closed her hand around the tiny light.

"Greetings, Starlight. Welcome to the Rainbow World. How may we be of service to you?"

Starlight smiled. The warmth that radiated through her fingers warmed her whole body.

"Hello, Rainbow," she replied. "I have come to ask if you and your fellow Rainbows would consider leaving your world."

A cloud passed over the sun then, dimming the light of the Rainbows, and Starlight sensed their sadness.

"I do not bring news of the demise of your planet, do not fear, Rainbows, for that is not what I am saying. Your planet will live on far beyond most others in the galaxy."

The sun came out again, and Starlight looked down at the Rainbow peeking through her fingers.

"We are pleased to hear that, Angel. What is it that you mean?"

"The beings on the planet called Earth are in trouble, and I am doing my best to help them change and survive. If they do manage to survive, then I wish for them to experience what is known Universally as the Golden Age."

"Yes, we understand. You wish for us to bring our light to their grey world."

Starlight was relieved that they had understood so quickly. "Yes, that's it exactly. At the moment, whether you will be needed or not is in doubt. The planet Earth may well be destroyed before you are able to go there. But I still have hope. Ultimately though, it is your decision. I will leave it up to you. If you should decide to go, then please go to the School for the Children of the Golden Age in the Fifth Dimension. I have already sent the Indigo and Crystal Children. They will be learning from the Angels and Faeries there before they are called to Earth."

"We shall need no teaching."

"I know, but as you are so wise, I was hoping your presence may help those going to Earth."

There was a pause, and Starlight felt a ripple in the air around her. A few moments later, the Rainbow spoke again.

"We have discussed the matter, and we shall go. But only if it appears as though we will be needed. We shall not leave our world unnecessarily."

Starlight smiled in relief. "Of course, that is all that I can ask of you. Thank you for speaking with me and agreeing to this."

"You are most welcome, Starlight. And from what we can feel, that uncertain future you have seen should be a little more certain now."

Starlight shook her head in wonder. She had not known of the Rainbows precognitive abilities.

"There is much that is unknown about us," the Rainbow whispered in reply.

Starlight opened her palm and the Rainbow danced away.

"Goodbye, Rainbows," she whispered softly. Then she closed her eyes and returned home.

*   *   *

Linen and Aria sat in the Angelic Garden in a state of shock.

"I can't believe she tried to leave," Aria whispered.

Linen shook his head. The image of Velvet's body lying on the sand would haunt him for the rest of his days. As much as he hated to admit it though, the fear he had felt when he'd found her was not that she had died, but that she had left him. Despite all of the work he had been doing, he still felt quite unprepared to take over the Academy when she was called to Earth and he was in charge.

"Do you think she'll be okay? I mean, do you think she'll be able to keep running the Academy?"

Linen sighed. "I hope so. There's still so much that I need to learn before she leaves. If I'm going to do half as good a job as she does, I need a bit more time."

"You'll be amazing," Aria patted Linen's hand and he jumped a little at the contact. "After all, if you weren't able to do the job, and do it well, the Angels would never have asked you to in the first place."

Linen looked up into Aria's sparkling green eyes and smiled. "You are absolutely right." He shook his head. "I've been doubting my ability to do this from the beginning, but I need to stop. They wouldn't have asked me if I was unable to do it. And I wouldn't have followed their instructions if at least part of me didn't think I could do it." He straightened up and put his hand on Aria's tiny shoulder. "Thank you."

Aria grinned and bounced up and down in the air. "You're welcome. Now, can we be a bit more cheerful? The events today have really killed my buzz."

Linen chuckled. "You're right. Velvet will be fine, I will be an amazing Head of the School and we are going to have a lot of fun."

"Now that's what I'm talking about!"

Despite Leon's prediction, Mica had found it difficult to stay in a positive state. He hated going to bed, knowing that in those few hours while he slept, Emerald was growing up fast and widening the gap between them. After yet another restless night, he lay in bed, staring at the ceiling. A tear formed in the corner of his eye.

He wondered where Emerald was, what she looked like, who she would become. He hoped that she had chosen a good family, one that would care for her, and nurture her, giving her the love that she would need to carry out her mission later in life.

He closed his eyes and the single tear hit his pillow. "I love you, Emerald, and I will find you."

"Mica."

For a moment he thought that she had heard his love through the dimensions of space and time that separated them, and was responding. But the Angelic voice didn't sound exactly like hers. Slowly, afraid to scare it away, he opened his eyes and sat up. He only had to wait silently for a few minutes before he heard his name the second time.

This time, the call penetrated his core and the joy bubbled up inside him.

He was being called.

Though he wanted to answer the call immediately, he knew he had to say goodbye to Velvet, after all, she had kept him going, given him comfort, and had been a wonderful teacher and friend.

He went to his morning class, only to find it had been cancelled. No one seemed to know why though. Every time he heard the call, his heart leapt, and he was desperate to answer it.

He wandered restlessly around the gardens, willing the

day to end so that it would be time for the evening class. The call was becoming louder and more insistent, and he knew he wouldn't be able to wait much longer, but he really couldn't leave without saying goodbye. Finally, the evening arrived and he went to the main hall again. He saw Velvet's purple robes by the doors to the hall and he rushed up to greet her.

*   *   *

After Velvet was safely back at the Academy, Gold returned to his post feeling agitated and not really understanding why. He had known that Velvet would return to the Academy, it was a part of the future that Starlight had shown him. But he still felt that she should have been allowed to stay in the Angelic Realm a bit longer. Perhaps he just felt guilty for the pain she had suffered, and felt that she deserved to be nurtured and looked after for a while. It seemed that she, like himself and Starlight, had spent her entire existence so far caring for others and never taking time for herself.

It wasn't as though they didn't have a choice in the matter though. This was the existence that they had all chosen to experience. They had chosen their roles in the Universe, so they could choose otherwise if they wanted to.

Gold sighed and shifted his weight from one foot to the other. Was that the problem? Had he rallied for Velvet's right to choose because he wanted to choose a different existence, but felt that he couldn't? He allowed that thought, that idea, rest with him for a while, and let it wash over him. It felt right.

Though he had chosen this path, willingly, he now wished that he could be just like any other being on Earth, or even on the Other Side. Be free to live, to love, to choose. That way, he could be with his own Twin Flame.

Gold sighed as he sensed an imminent arrival in the form of a child. He would have to set aside his own thoughts and feelings to help the soul. After all, that was what he was here to do. That was the existence he had chosen.

It was a pity that when he chose this path, he hadn't realised that in doing so, he had given up his own right to free will.

*   *   *

"Hello, Mica."

Mica's face broke out into a grin. "Hello, Angel!" He stepped forwards and engulfed the petite Angel in a hug. "It's so good to see you, I really cannot tell you. I have been desperate to hear the call since Emerald left."

The Guardian Angel stepped back and smiled widely. "We know. We did not separate you out of malice, Angel, please know that."

Mica nodded. "I know. It was hard to accept and to live with, but I understand that there are good reasons for it."

"You are a wise Angel, Mica. I shall be your guide and guardian while you are on planet Earth. If you ever need any assistance, please do not hesitate to call to me."

"I will, Angel, I will. Thank you. Can I go now?"

The Guardian Angel chuckled. "You already know your mission on Earth?"

"Of course. To find Emerald and reunite the Flames. It is our joint mission."

The Guardian Angel smiled. "Very well, then yes, you are free to begin your new life. Peace, love and light be with you always."

"And with you." Mica closed his eyes and left the mists to begin his quest to find his Flame.

*   *   *

Cobalt was waiting on a red and white toadstool when Amethyst arrived in the Elemental Garden that evening. He hopped off and met her on the cobbled path.

Before even uttering a word, he leaned in and kissed her softly. She melted into his embrace and he held her body close to his, imprinting the emotions he felt into his soul.

"Good evening to you too," she whispered when they finally stopped.

Cobalt grinned. "I don't think I'd ever tire of kissing you, Angel. Or looking into your eyes, or feeling your hand in mine."

Amethyst smiled. "I feel the same way. How did we manage to exist up until this moment without each other?"

"I have no idea." Cobalt took her hand and they began to walk along the path. "But I do know that my senses were dull before the moment we met."

"Mine too. I must confess as well, that despite my inner knowing that I would one day meet my Flame, there were moments in time when I doubted it. When I thought that perhaps it might not happen."

Cobalt's grip on her hand tightened. "Destiny is such a fragile thing, isn't it? I watched Earth from the Angelic Realm, and I saw the webs of connection between souls and I knew which souls matched, and which didn't. But there was nothing I could do to nudge them in the right direction."

"I know what you mean, I felt such sadness, waiting for them to ask me for help. Knowing that I could change everything for them in an instant."

"When I get to Earth, I will make sure I ask the Angels for help every day in finding you. I will not rest until we are together again."

Amethyst stopped and reached up to kiss him. A few souls passed them on the path, chattering loudly. "Shall we go somewhere a little more private?"

Cobalt smiled. "You must have read my thoughts. Shall we go to the Leprechaun Garden? Now that we know how to get there?"

Amethyst nodded and hand in hand they set off towards the secret entrance.

*   *   *

Linen sat at his desk after Velvet, Aria and Cotton left, feeling a little shocked. One of the first-year Starpeople had been called. Linen knew that he was working to a tight schedule, because the Indigo Child had told him things would be moving quickly, but he hadn't imagined that the first-year trainees would begin to be called so soon.

He looked at the papers covering his desk; the schedules, brochures and interview notes and felt panic rising up within him. He wished Aria hadn't gone with Velvet and Cotton. She always knew what to say to calm him down, to make him feel like he really was up to this huge task.

Unable to begin to organise his paperwork or his thoughts, Linen got up from his desk and moved to the piano. He hadn't played it since the incident with Tartan, but he felt the need to play now, to get lost in the music for a while, and forget all of the responsibility that was weighing him down. As soon as his fingers hit the keys, his shoulders relaxed. He closed his eyes and allowed himself to play without guidance or direction, and after a few moments of random notes, a melody began to form, one that he had not heard before.

After a few minutes, his fingers became still on the keys and the last note hovered in the air.

"That was beautiful."

He opened his eyes and looked up to see Velvet standing in the doorway. "Thank you."

"What was it? I don't think I've ever heard it before."

Linen shrugged. "I have no idea. I just closed my eyes and it came through me."

Velvet crossed the office and sat down behind her desk. "Was it effortless?"

Linen nodded. "Completely."

"Were you worried about making mistakes?"

"No, I just hit the keys randomly until a pattern began to emerge and it started to sound like music."

Velvet smiled. "Then why are you so afraid of making mistakes with the School, Linen?"

Linen's eyes widened. "How did you know?"

"I can tell. Old Souls know everything, remember? Running the School will be effortless, as long as you just allow things to happen, and keep going until it begins to come together."

"You're right." Linen looked down at the keys of the piano. "It's just that it's such a huge responsibility. You seem to do it all so effortlessly, but I don't think I-"

"Linen. I have been doing my job for a long time. Do you think it was effortless in the beginning? Do you think I found it easy? Do you think it all worked out perfectly? Of course not. But I had faith that everything would begin to harmonise, and that it would work out perfectly in the end."

Linen got up from the piano and went back to his desk. He began to sort through the paperwork, and organise it into piles, figuring out what needed to be done next. He looked up to see Velvet watching him.

"If you need any help, you can ask me, you know."

He smiled. "Thank you, Velvet. But I think I have it under control now."

"Very well. I'm going to retire for the evening. It's been another busy day." She stood up. "I'm still in shock that one of the first-years was called this evening."

"Me too. Did he go okay?"

"Yes, once I explained that he was being called, he answered and left immediately. I think he'll be just fine. The Starpeople of Zubenelgenubi seem to adapt to being human more easily than some of the other Starpeople."

"That's good."

"Good night, Linen, please do get some rest. There is still time to organise everything, I promise."

"Aria and I need to visit the Angelic Realm tomorrow, to hire our Angel teachers."

"I will be here first thing, so I can help you get there."

"Thank you. Good night, Velvet."

With a nod, Velvet clicked her fingers and disappeared, leaving Linen staring at the paperwork again. He picked out what he needed for the morning, and left it on the top. Then he decided to go for a walk in the gardens, before trying to get some rest.

*   *   *

Starlight observed the events at the Academy with a smile. Everything was coming together perfectly, just as Velvet had told Linen that it would. A perfect harmony. She found it amusing that Velvet still had no idea who she really was.

Velvet was the Angel of Fate. A long time ago, they had decided that she should give up her wings, and become human. That she could achieve so much more to shape the fate of each civilisation if she were part of it, rather than if she stayed like Starlight, a separate entity, hovering between worlds. So Starlight had said goodbye to her sister, and wished her luck with her mission.

She hadn't spoken with her since. She knew that she could visit the Academy any time she wished, but she kept her distance because she had foreseen what would happen if Velvet knew that there was another option. That she didn't have to struggle anymore, that she could go home, where she belonged. It was so important for Velvet to stay. And even more important for her to go to Earth to assist with the Awakening. She had been instrumental in the shifts that had happened in all of the previous ages. Starlight remembered the end of Atlantis. When Velvet had Seen the end, she had asked for help to save the people of Atlantis, so Starlight had visited her in a dream and told her how to turn them into Merpeople, so that they could take to the seas, and survive the end of their age.

Starlight knew that it would drain Velvet, she knew that it would kill her and her unborn child, yet she had done it anyway. Because that was her job. And helping the people of Atlantis to make the transition and continue living, was Velvet's job.

It had still been tough to watch. And Starlight didn't think that it would be any easier to watch Velvet's path this time, either. The future that had been flickering was becoming clearer and more certain, which gave Starlight hope that despite everything, it would turn out well in the end.

She turned her attention to the progress of the Crystal Children. It had taken them a while to travel from their planet, but they were very nearly there. Once the Crystal Children were at the Academy, things would begin to move very quickly.

Chapter Fourteen

On his way to class that morning, Leon overheard that one of the trainees had been called. It had almost stopped him in his tracks. He nearly went back to the soul and asked them if he had heard them correctly, but he felt it was a little rude to do so. When he arrived at his Human Emotions class, now run by a guest professor, since Professor Indigo had left, he heard more whispers, confirming what he'd heard.

"I will be teaching a different class to what was planned today, as I have been asked by Velvet to explain the process you will go through when you are called to Earth." The professor, an Old Soul called Calico, clicked her fingers and a machine appeared in front of her on the table. The trainees all leaned closer to see what it was. It looked like a very strange contraption to Leon.

"Seeing as the call can be heard by no other than the one who is being called, and is in the mind, it therefore cannot be recorded. But so that you will understand what is happening, we asked the Angels to replicate what it sounds like."

Filix, a former Faerie, put his hand up. Calico nodded for him to speak.

"Is it true that one of the trainees was called last night?" he asked.

Leon noticed that Amethyst, who was sat next to him, was

nodding. He wondered if the one who had been called was a friend of hers.

"Yes," Calico said. "It is true. A Starperson from Zubenelgenubi was called to Earth late last night. But it was a much more traumatic experience for him than it should have been, because he did not understand what was happening."

Filix's hand shot up again

"Yes, Filix?"

"Does that mean we will all be called soon? It just seems like we've only been here a very short time, isn't it too soon? Won't we fail in our missions if we go now?"

Leon heard the fear in Filix's voice and he felt bad for his fellow Faerie. He was so glad that he had his Sight to comfort him. If he had not Seen the things he had, he knew he would be filled with such fears too.

"I believe that you will each be called at the exact moment that is perfect for you to leave for Earth. You shall not be called before you are ready. Tim was ready to leave for Earth, he was only afraid because he did not understand the process." Before Filix could ask another question, Calico gestured to the black contraption next to her. "I would like you all to close your eyes, and listen. I am going to play this recording of what it will sound like when you are called to Earth."

Everyone closed their eyes, and after a moment, Leon joined them.

There was silence for a moment, then very softly, Leon heard his name. His eyes popped open, and he nearly answered, but he looked around and saw that everyone else still had their eyes closed. He looked up and saw Calico smile at him and motion for him to close his eyes again. As soon as he did, his name was called a second time, it was a little louder than the first. Within minutes, he heard it again, this time though, it was as though there were two voices.

Half an hour later, Leon had tears running down his cheeks. The sound of a million Angels all calling his name had given him chills. He hoped that it wouldn't be long before he heard the call for real. He opened his eyes and wiped his face with his sleeve, noticing a few of his classmates doing the same thing.

He raised his hand and Calico smiled at him. "Why did you choose my name as the name for them to call?" he asked, his voice rough.

Calico shook her head. "I didn't. This is a very special device. Upon listening to the recording of the Angels, the listener will hear their own name."

Leon's eyes widened. "So we each heard our own names being called?" He looked around the room and everyone was nodding. He sat back in his chair, in awe of the possibilities that existed.

"Now that you know what it feels like and sounds like to be called, I hope it will be a beautiful experience when it happens for you."

Amethyst raised her hand before speaking. "Will we get any other warning before being called?"

"No, the first sign you'll have will be the one Angel calling your name."

"Must we answer immediately?" Amethyst asked, a look of concern on her face.

"No, you can answer the call once you are ready to leave. Of course, as you heard from the recording, the call becomes quite intense. It would be difficult for you to resist answering for very long. But you should have long enough to say goodbye to your friends, to perhaps visit your favourite place for a while, or indeed say goodbye to a Flame."

Leon noticed that Amethyst blushed a little and looked sad at the same time. He wondered if she had met her Flame already. He had not met his, and he had not yet Seen himself with his Flame either. But that didn't mean that he was not fated to meet them. If his life was to be entangled with Velvet and Laguz's then he was sure that meeting his own Flame must be on the cards.

At least, he hoped so.

*   *   *

"Are you sure that trainees aren't going to be called immediately?"

Linen sighed and wished he could take away the sad look on Aria's face. "I really do not know, Aria. I should think that they will only be called when they are ready, and I really doubt that many of the trainees are ready yet." Despite his reassuring tones, he really wasn't sure if what he said was true. He did know that Tm's departure had scared him a little. Things were moving so quickly.

Aria thought about his words for a moment. "So you really think Tim was ready to leave?"

"I'm sure of it."

Aria smiled, and all of the tension in her little body disappeared. "Okay. So where are we going today?"

Linen smiled, pleased that she seemed comforted by his words. "We need to go to the Angelic Realm today. I think it would be best if we choose five Angels we want to hire today, and then go back to the Elemental Realm for the second interviews and decide on five from the seven we liked." He looked over his notes. "We're going to run out of time if we don't do this quickly, I would like to have a few sessions with the teachers before they have to conduct classes for the Children."

Aria nodded. "I can't wait to visit the Angels! Are we leaving now?"

Linen chuckled. "Yes, though we will have to wait for Velvet, she will need to send us there. I really must learn the Old Soul Magick so that we can get around easily when Velvet has gone."

"Oooh, can you learn how to do the clicky trick thing?"

Linen smiled. "I hope so." He tucked all of the paperwork he needed into his case.

"Good morning, both!"

Aria and Linen looked up at Velvet who had appeared behind her desk.

"Good morning, Velvet. Would you mind getting us to the Angelic Realm?"

Velvet nodded. "Of course. Just take each other's hands."

Aria flew over to Linen and he took her tiny hand in his. He picked up his case and they both closed their eyes, waiting for the click.

"Greetings, Linen, Aria."

Linen opened his eyes and reluctantly released Aria's hand. He smiled at the Angel.

"Hello, Pearl. We've come to do the interviews. I trust that the recruitment office informed you we were coming?"

"Of course. The Angels to be interviewed are waiting for you." She gestured towards the gates, which opened automatically, sweeping back the white mists that swirled around the invisible floor.

Linen and Aria entered the Angelic Realm, and an Angel appeared to guide them.

"Welcome, my name is Carnelian."

"Hi, Carnelian!" Aria said, liking the Angel immediately. "Are you one of the Angels we are interviewing today?"

Carnelian smiled but shook her head. "No, little Faerie. I am just showing you the way. I will be staying here in the Angelic Realm for a while longer yet."

"Oh," Aria said. "Well I guess some Angels have to stay here, otherwise there'd be no one to help the humans when they ask for it."

"Indeed."

Aria and Linen followed the Angel down the path to a beautiful circular building. They both looked in awe at the gold detailing, the seamless way it was constructed, and the way it gleamed. In the distance beyond the building, they could see a lake, with Angels sat around the edges.

"Can we visit the lake after the interviews?" Aria asked.

Carnelian smiled and gestured for them to enter the building. "Of course, little one. The lake is our way of watching Earth. Upon its surface, the lives of those on Earth can be seen, witnessed, and if they ask us to, we can help them."

"Wow, that's so cool! I definitely want to see. Is that okay, Linen?"

Linen smiled at Aria, but could feel his stress creeping back in. "If we have time, sure. But we really need to focus on finding the right teachers today."

Aria immediately snapped to attention and followed him into the building. "Of course! I only meant if there was time after." She looked around and gasped. It was even more heavenly and beautiful inside. In the room they entered, several Angels were milling about.

"Greetings, my dear friends and family. Linen and Aria of the School for the Children of the Golden Age have arrived."

The Angels all turned to look at Linen and Aria and some waved, some clapped and some bowed their heads in greeting. Aria waved back enthusiastically.

"There is a room through there," Carnelian pointed to a door on their right. "Here are the candidates' names." She handed Linen a gold-edged parchment scroll. "Good luck, I hope you find the right teachers for your School."

"Thank you, Carnelian." Linen took the paper and headed for the door.

Aria hung back for a moment. "Are you sure you don't want to join the School? You'd make a fantastic teacher."

Carnelian chuckled. "I am quite sure, young one. But thank you." She turned and flew out the door, and Aria shrugged and followed Linen. She went inside and they settled into the upholstered golden chairs that had been set out for them. Aria sank into the plush fabric and sighed. "It really is quite beautiful here. So fancy and pretty and so much cleaner than the Elemental Realm."

Linen chuckled. "Yes, well, they can manifest anything they wish, so why would they manifest anything shabby or dirty?"

"True. So, who's up first? I'll go call them in."

Linen checked the paper. "Citrine."

Aria flew to the door and called out into the foyer. "Citrine!"

A moment later, a beautiful Angel with yellow robes flew into the room, and settled into the oversized chair opposite them.

"So, Citrine, why would you like to be a teacher at the School?"

*   *   *

"Aria is so worried about me leaving now. Ever since Tim was called, she wakes up every morning calling my name, as if she's afraid I will have disappeared during the night."

Cobalt squeezed Amethyst's hand. "Poor Faerie, doesn't she realise that soon we will all be called, and she will just be here with Linen and the Children? I mean, that's the plan isn't it?"

"I think she knows that, but hasn't fully taken in the implications. Though I imagine that she will have no objections to having Linen all to herself."

Cobalt looked over at Amethyst, her flowing lilac robes contrasted beautifully against the bed of bright green clover they were sitting in. "They're Flames, aren't they?"

"Yes, they are. And it amazes me that neither of them has figured it out yet. I knew, the instant I met you, that we were connected." Amethyst smiled and leaned over to kiss him. He received the kiss and lingered, breathing in her lavender scent.

- 143 -

"I knew it too," he said, looking into her eyes. "I knew that you were the reason I felt compelled to come to the Academy. I didn't know my reason for being until I bumped into you in the hallway." He kissed her then, wishing that he could stay forever in the Leprechaun Garden, with Amethyst in his arms, watching the rainbows appear and disappear.

"Do you think it will be long before you are called?" Amethyst whispered.

Cobalt could hear the fear in her voice, and his chest tightened. "I don't know," he replied honestly. "Though I am enjoying the classes with Velvet, there is nothing important I feel I need to learn before going." He smoothed her blonde hair back. "I think the only reason I came to the Academy was to meet you and to understand what it was like to be with my Flame, and therefore have a reason to help people to Awaken when I get to Earth."

Amethyst nodded. "I'm glad that we have experienced this love. It will help a lot, knowing deep in our souls that it is possible to experience such bliss."

"Yes it will. I hope that we get to have a while longer with one another. I'm not quite ready to leave you yet."

Amethyst rested her head on his shoulder. "I'm not ready to lose you yet, either."

They sat in companionable silence for a while, before Cobalt broke the quiet.

"It's getting late, we have classes this afternoon."

Amethyst sighed. "Yes. I suppose we should make a move."

Cobalt stood and held a hand out to Amethyst. She took it and he pulled her to her feet. They walked down the path paved with gold coins towards the exit.

Just before they reached it, Cobalt stopped and pulled Amethyst close to him. "There's something I need to say."

"What is it?"

"I love you." Though he had said the words in many of his

previous lifetimes, he had never felt it so deeply before, it had never been so true, so deep, and so absolute.

"I love you, too." Amethyst closed her eyes and Cobalt leaned down to kiss her. He knew he would never forget the feeling of her lips, her scent, or her touch. It was imprinted on his soul.

Chapter Fifteen

"It's really very simple, Linen. Though we call it the Old Soul Magick, really, any being can master it. Old Souls just find it easier to do so, that's all."

Linen nodded at Chiffon, who had agreed to teach him how to travel wherever he wished with the click of his fingers. "So what do you do?"

"There are three steps. First, you set your intention. Which is to travel instantaneously to the place you wish to go to. Then the second step is to visualise that place. To see it in your mind's eye. The third and last step is to know, with absolute faith and conviction that you are already there." Chiffon smiled at Linen's raised eyebrows. "The reason that Old Souls find this easy to do, is that they know that time and space really doesn't exist, and that we are everywhere and nowhere and here and there all at once. So the part of knowing with absolute faith and conviction that they are in the place they wish to be is easy for them."

Linen nodded slowly. "Okay, I understand the steps, and it does sound simple, but I'm not sure whether I'll be able to do it."

Chiffon shook her head. "In that case you won't. You need absolute conviction for it to work, remember?"

Linen sighed. "Of course. So, my intention should be to move instantaneously to where I visualise, and then know absolutely that I am already there?"

"Yes. That's right."

"What if I have never been there before? What if I cannot visualise it?"

"Good question. Well, as you saw when we found Velvet, I did not know where she was, so I simply visualised her and set the intention to move to wherever she currently was. Though because I was visualising her body, that is what we found."

"So you can find people by visualising where they are."

"Yes, though it takes a little more concentration, because, of course people are constantly moving."

"Got it. So what do we do now?"

Chiffon stood and motioned for Linen to do the same. "We practice, of course. The theory is fine, but we need to try it out. Where do you like to spend time in the Academy, somewhere that you can visualise in great detail?"

"The Elemental Garden," Linen replied, getting to his feet.

"Very well. Set the intention to move there, then visualise it, a specific spot if possible. You can close your eyes if it's easier."

Linen closed his eyes and pictured the giant toadstool he enjoyed sitting on. He pictured the surroundings, the flowers, the path winding past, the dragonflies hovering about.

"Now know, with absolute faith and certainty, that you are already there," Chiffon whispered. Linen felt her hand on his shoulder. Then he heard her click her fingers.

He opened his eyes and looked around in amazement. They were in the exact spot that he had visualised, standing right next to his favourite toadstool. "That's amazing!" He reached out to touch the leathery red oversized fungi and smiled. "We're really here."

"And you were the one who got us here."

"I didn't click my fingers though, you did."

Chiffon waved her hand dismissively. "The clicking of the

fingers is simply a focusing tool. Instead of a magic wand or staff, it provides a point of focus, and acts as a trigger of sorts. Really, it is the mental work that you did that moved us from my office to this garden."

"Can we try to move back?"

"Of course. This time, I will say nothing, and do nothing. You will just take me along for the ride."

Linen nodded and closed his eyes. He felt Chiffon's hand on his shoulder again. He set his intention, then he pictured the inside of Chiffon's office, where they had been stood just minutes before. He pictured the orange decor, the soft furnishings and her ornate desk. Then he decided, with conviction this time, that they were already there. Then he clicked his fingers. After a moment, he opened one eye, and a dragonfly sped past. Chiffon still stood opposite him in the garden, her eyes closed, and a serene look on her face. He took a deep breath, went through the steps again, and clicked his fingers with a little more force this time.

"Well done, Linen."

He opened his eyes and saw that they were back in Chiffon's office. He grinned at her in relief. "I can do it!"

"Of course you can. Now try to apply that absolute faith and conviction to yourself and your own abilities, and you will truly be unstoppable." Chiffon winked then returned to her desk and sat.

"Thank you, Chiffon." Linen went to leave her office through the door, but then had another idea. He closed his eyes, set the intention to be in his room, visualised it, then clicked his fingers.

When he opened his eyes to find himself stood next to his bed, he let out a very Faerie-like squeal and jumped up and down in excitement. Then he shook himself, took a deep breath, and returned to his new, serious self.

But as he left his room he couldn't help but grin all the way to the office.

Starlight answered the call and was there in a heartbeat.

"Yes, Gold?"

Gold looked up, a strained smile on his face. "Things are progressing rather more quickly than I imagined, Starlight. Is everything still on course for the future you have chosen, or have things changed?"

Starlight detected the hint of hope in his voice and smiled. "Everything is working out as it was intended, Gold. All those concerned are on the right path. This is the speed in which it was meant to happen. Earth is in decline and if things don't progress rapidly here, then all of our efforts will be for nothing."

"I see. One thing that has been puzzling me, I must admit, is if time is running out on Earth, why have you speeded it up? Wouldn't it have been better to have a whole year's training here in this dimension for each day that passes on Earth? That way, we could have trained and sent several classes of Earth Angels to Earth within a few weeks."

Starlight sighed. "Logically, that would have made a whole lot more sense. But then as you know, we live in a creative Universe, not a logical one. The reasons for changing the timescale were less to do with common sense and more to do with the way the mind works."

"You have lost me."

Starlight smiled. "It is necessary for those whose Flames have left before them to think that perhaps they will not get to meet, because there will too many years between them."

"And that is necessary because?"

"Because then they will be more determined to find them. They will be more passionate, more focused, and more driven. And that is exactly the kind of Earth Angel the world needs. If they are too complacent, then the reunion of the Flames may not happen on as a big a scale as we hope for."

"You really do see every facet, every possibility, don't you? How is it that I was unable to see this for myself?"

"Because you are trying to be too sensible, Gold. You need to release your creative power and think from there. But it was a fair question. I am surprised that no one else so far has questioned it."

"I think they are just dealing with the consequences of it, rather than wondering about the sanity of it."

"It would seem that most humans operate in that way. Which is not necessarily a bad thing. Though questioning the reason behind big decisions is always a good idea."

"Indeed." Gold stepped forwards and hugged her. "Thank you for coming, Starlight. I am sorry that I have distracted you from your duties."

"It is always my pleasure to visit, Gold. I always have time for you, you know that."

"Thank you. I look forward to seeing you again soon."

Starlight smiled then closed her eyes and returned home.

*   *   *

"I think we made good choices with the Angels. Though it's a shame that we couldn't hire them all," Aria said, looking at the list of the Angel teachers they had chosen.

Linen nodded. "Yes, there were a couple of others I thought would have been great, but we can always hire them if we are in need of more teachers than we expect. After all, things have changed so much, who knows what might happen next? To be honest, at the moment, for the number of Children we have, I think that the recruiting souls may have overestimated the number of teachers we need. I think we have too many."

"We can't change our minds now! We've already told them they can come and be teachers!"

Linen patted Aria's hand. "It's okay, Faerie, calm. I won't go back on our decisions now, it wouldn't be fair. We're just going to have very small classes, that's all."

"That's not a bad thing. It's better than the huge classes that Velvet is having to teach at the moment. I'm sure the Children will learn more this way."

"I'm sure you are right." Linen set his papers down and sighed. "I don't think I can do anymore work. Shall we call it a day? It is getting late."

"Sure." Aria set down her work too and flew up from her chair. "Do you want to do anything? Or are you going to go to bed?"

"I thought I might play the piano for a while, actually."

"Ooooh! Can I listen?"

Linen smiled. "Sure. I only know a few tunes. I've been making some up though."

"Awesome." Aria settled back on her chair and Linen moved to the piano stool. He sat and opened the gleaming white grand piano. After hovering above the keys for a second, his fingers softly touched down, and Linen closed his eyes and began to play, not entirely sure what the melody would sound like until he heard it.

He remembered their trip to the Elemental Realm, and the Angelic Realm, and the notes reflected the joyfulness of the Faeries, the speed of the Sparrow Express, the absolute pleasure of seeing Aria and Larry reunited, and then the calm of the Angelic Realm. Throughout the song, he could see Aria's face, her sparkling green eyes, her mischievous grin and her beautiful wings. When his fingers came to a standstill, he hadn't even opened his eyes when he heard the enthusiastic clapping of tiny hands.

"Wow! Linen that was incredible!" Aria flew over to him and put her tiny arms around his neck to hug him. He blushed red at her touch. "What was it called?"

Linen shook his head. "It doesn't have a name."

"You mean you just made that up? That's so cool!"

Linen laughed. "It's easy here, like I am connected to the Universal energy and the music just flows through me. Perhaps we should call that one 'Aria'."

Now it was Aria's turn to blush bright red. "Really? You're going to name it after me?"

Linen shrugged, now feeling a bit shy. "You inspired it. I was thinking of our trip to the Elemental and Angelic Realms when I was playing it."

"Wow," Aria said softly. "I've never had a song named after me. I think that's the most amazing thing ever."

Linen smiled. "I think I need to go to bed. It's been a very busy day."

"Yes it has, you're right. Good night, Linen." Aria headed for the door of the office.

"Good night, Aria," Linen responded, watching her leave. Even though he knew he would see her the very next day, as the door reappeared behind her, Linen suddenly felt empty and bereft. Though he had tried hard to deny it, he knew that his feelings for the small green Faerie were far deeper and stronger than they would be if she were just a colleague. He had no idea what it was like to be with a soulmate, having only reached the age of ten on Earth and having spent his entire life before that as a lone fire Faerie in the Elemental Realm. But he wondered if it felt like he did right then. Like she was a part of him. Another part of his soul.

He wanted to ask Velvet, but he had been avoiding the whole subject of Twin Flames and soulmates since Laguz had left. It seemed too cruel to talk about it, when she was missing her own Flame so much.

Linen sighed and closed the piano. He guessed he would just have to wait and see what happened. He headed out of the office, and back to his room, to get some rest before the next day's madness began.

The first time he saw her, he gasped out loud. Luckily, he was alone in the Elemental Garden when the vision appeared, otherwise he might have startled someone.

He watched her move towards him, a smile on her face, her hands outstretched, reaching for him. He widened his Sight to take in their surroundings, and saw that they were in a café in a busy city. He looked at the buildings but he didn't know where it was on Earth.

In his vision, Leon took her hand, and her smile grew. "I've been waiting for you."

Leon blinked in shock. It wasn't often that he could hear anything during his visions. Mostly it was just snapshots, sometimes it was a moving image, but this was the first time he had heard the voice of someone he could See in the future.

"I'm sorry I made you wait," he whispered back.

She shook her head. "You're worth it."

Leon smiled and before he could reply, she was gone.

He blinked and looked around him. The Elemental Garden looked exactly like it had a few moments before, except that the colours were a little brighter, more vivid and intense. He had just seen his Flame. He was sure of it. And judging from her flowing hair, curvy body and bright blue eyes, she was a Mermaid. Her body seemed to be dancing in unseen waves as she had reached out to him.

Two souls passed by on the path, their quiet chattering making Leon jump a little. He looked up and recognised the lilac coloured robes and blonde hair of his classmate, Amethyst. He didn't recognise her companion, but deduced from their postures and their soft words that he was her Flame. He watched them pass, and was hit with another vision.

He saw Amethyst's life on Earth like a movie that had been sped up. He saw her meet one man after another, searching for her Flame. He saw her have children, being mistreated, yet still following her calling to help others in their Awakening. He saw her write books, which inspired people. Finally, he saw her find her Flame. The vision slowed down and he saw the recognition in their eyes when they met for the first time. He saw their bodies and lives entwine, and the vision faded away.

He blinked and realised that the voices had gone, and he was alone in the garden again. A tear slid down his cheek as he thought of the years Amethyst would spend without her Flame, and he wondered if he should warn her, and urge her to cherish every moment spent with him now.

But it wasn't really his place to do so. He knew, though it was hard, that she would have to go through the tough times on Earth so that she could complete her missions.

His thoughts wandered back to his own Flame and he sighed. He could only hope that he would meet her before he became too old. He had been a loner for far too long, and he looked forward to the day he would be wrapped in the embrace of his true mate.

*　　　*　　　*

"Linen! I have an urgent message for you."

Linen looked up at Beryl who was standing in the doorway.

"Sure, what is it?" He got up to greet her and she handed him a note. He took it and his eyes widened when he saw the almost translucent paper with writing that appeared to glow. It was simple and to the point.

"Dear Head of the School for the Children of the Golden Age. We shall be arriving shortly in Room 334. Please come to greet us at your earliest convenience. Thank you."

Linen looked up at Beryl. "Who is arriving in room 334?"

Beryl shook her head. "I know as much as you do, the note just appeared on my desk."

"When did it arrive?"

"Not long ago. Should I call Velvet to assist you?"

Linen shook his head and set the note on his desk. "It's okay, I'll go to room 334, and if I need any help from Velvet, I will find her."

"Don't forget you have a meeting with the new teachers at 12.30pm," Beryl reminded him.

Linen smiled, thankful that even though she was not his secretary, she helped to keep him on schedule at times.

"I know, hopefully this won't take long. Thank you, Beryl."

Beryl nodded and retreated from the room. Linen closed his eyes and visualised room 333, then clicked his fingers. Having visited the Indigos a few times now, he knew he would be able to get there okay.

He appeared in front of room 333, and turned to face the door to 334, pausing for a moment before entering. He had no idea what would be inside. He took a deep breath, squared his shoulders, and told himself that he could handle anything. After all, he was the Head of the School for the Children of the Golden Age. The door disappeared and he stepped in. The room was dim so he muttered quietly for the room to lighten. When he saw what stood before him, his eyes widened and he gasped.

Before him was a sea of crystals. Massive crystals of all shapes, sizes and colours, standing in rows. They glittered softly in the light he had created. After a few moments, he cleared his throat.

"Um, welcome!" he said. He waited for a reply but there was none. They stood silently, as though they were just watching him. After a few minutes he realised that he was getting short on time if he was to get to the meeting with the teachers, so he decided it would be a good idea to find Velvet. Perhaps she would know what to do. He closed his eyes and visualised Velvet. He knew it was harder to transport himself to where a specific person was, as opposed to a specific place,

- 156 -

but he wanted to try it out. Once he had a clear picture of Velvet in his mind, he clicked his fingers.

*   *   *

"As much as I love being in the gardens, how about we go back to my room for a while?" Amethyst suggested as she and Cobalt walked through the Underwater Garden. Her hair flowed around her like a halo in the invisible current and Cobalt smiled.

"Will we be alone?" As much as he liked the little green Faerie, Aria, she was a little too excitable for Cobalt. He much preferred the serenity of Amethyst's company.

"I should think so. Aria isn't around much, and of course Tim is now on Earth. I just thought it might be a little more comfortable there."

Cobalt nodded and followed Amethyst's lead in heading back to the Academy and to her room. When they reached room 409, he paused outside the door. "Maybe you should check first."

Amethyst chuckled. "I know Aria is a little crazy, but she's not so bad." She entered the room and glanced around. The room was quiet, a sure sign that Aria was definitely not present.

She popped her head back out into the corridor. "It's safe," she stage-whispered, a grin on her face.

Cobalt smiled back and let her pull him inside. Once enclosed in the room, he pulled her into his arms and kissed her deeply. Despite being within the Academy, surrounded by hundreds of souls, it felt like they were completely alone.

He pulled back and stared at her face for a few seconds, her eyes still closed, her lips still slightly pursed. He would never tire of looking at her, not even if he stayed there with her for the rest of eternity.

She opened her eyes and smiled when she caught him

staring. "What are you thinking?"

"I was thinking that I could spend eternity just looking at you."

Amethyst blushed. "Thank you."

Cobalt pulled Amethyst towards what he assumed was her bed and they lay side by side on top of the covers, their bodies melting together. "I just hope we find each other again."

Amethyst tightened her grip on his hand. "We have to. We belong together."

"Yes, we do." Cobalt breathed in the lavender scent of her hair and closed his eyes. Though he was an Angel, and had lived in the Angelic Realm, before that moment, he had not truly understood what bliss was.

Chapter Sixteen

"Thank you all for coming, and for accepting the offer of teaching at the School for the Children of the Golden Age." Linen looked around the circle of Angels and Faeries that he and Aria had chosen, and smiled at each of them in turn. "I appreciate that it was a big decision to leave your home to come here and teach classes at a brand new establishment to Children that you know nothing of, so thank you."

There was a murmur around the circle as the beings acknowledged his words. Aria bounced up and down in her seat next to him, making him smile.

"The purpose of today's meeting is for us to share with you what we know of the Children so far, to let you know what we have arranged in terms of classes, and the subjects that we feel should be taught. We will invite each of you in turn to share your thoughts on this, as Aria and I very much want to run the School as a team, a collective. Not in the same way the Academy currently runs. Everyone will have equal say, regardless of any titles."

"Because we're all the same! Linen and I aren't any better than any of you because we were here first."

Linen chuckled, as did a few of the Faeries. "Thank you, Aria. You're right. The first stage of the Golden Age Children to arrive, were the Indigo Children. All we know about them so far is that they have a very high vibrational energy, and they are going to Earth to help to change the systems currently in place that educate Children there. There are roughly a hundred of them, and until called, they remain in their Golden City as small blue spheres of light."

A small iridescent blue Faerie raised her hand. Linen nodded for her to speak. "There are only a hundred? If that is the case, why are there so many of us?"

"Patience, Faerie. Today, just a very short while ago, another group of Children arrived at the Academy. They are known as the Crystal Children. And there are at least two hundred of them."

"Crystal Children?" an Angel called Citrine asked.

"Yes, they arrived in their natural crystal state. There is apparently to be three stages of the Golden Age Children. The Indigos are the first, the Crystals are the second, and as yet we do not know who will be the third." He looked around the room. "Are there any questions?"

Another Faerie put her hand up. "Will we be choosing our names today?"

"Ooooh, Linen, can they?" Aria asked, bouncing up and down enthusiastically. "Choosing my name was so much fun!"

"Of course, it would make sense to do so, after all, we need to be able to introduce you all properly to the Children."

"Can I go first?" A small Faerie with butterfly wings asked, so excited she didn't bother to raise her hand first.

Aria smiled at the Faerie. "Sure! What is your favourite flower?"

"It's a tree, is that okay?"

"Sure."

"I used to look after an orange tree. I love the smell!"

Aria smiled and looked at Linen. "That's great, the Latin name for the orange tree is, um," she looked at Linen, hoping he would fill in the blank.

Linen's eyes widened. He had no idea what the Latin names of the trees or flowers were, nor had he thought to study them. He closed his eyes briefly, and opened his awareness to connect to the Universal energy. "It's Aurantium." His eyes popped open and he smiled at the Faerie. He looked at Aria who was looking simultaneously relieved and impressed.

"Aurantium," the Faerie repeated. "I like it! Could I shorten it to Aura?"

"I shortened mine!" Aria said. "My full name is Lunaria."

"It is your name to do with as you wish." Linen turned to the next Faerie. "What is your favourite tree or flower?"

The male Faerie wearing brown leaves smiled. "Mine is a tree also, the oak."

"I know this one! The Latin name is Quercus!" Aria grinned, looking pleased with herself.

"Quercus. That's perfect. I will keep it as is."

Linen nodded and moved onto the Angel sat next to him. "And of course, you are Citrine," the Angel nodded. "And then we have Turquoise, Jade, Herkimer and Copper. Welcome, Angels." The Angels all nodded and smiled.

Once the final three teachers, all Faeries, were named, Linen outlined the plan that he had for the School so far.

"I know that each of you have your own special interests, so rather than trying to name each class that you teach, I thought a more organic approach would be better. We will split the Children into groups, and then just rotate them from one teacher to another."

Everyone nodded. "Is there a specific focus for our teachings?" Herkimer asked.

"The main focus will be on how to remain connected, stay in a higher vibration, and about helping others and caring for the planet. The Indigo Children's primary focus is to change the systems on Earth. Especially the educational systems. The current systems are not teaching Children on Earth what they will need to know for the shift to happen. We do not know much about the Crystal Children yet."

"What are they like? The Indigo Children?" the pink

Faerie, Fraggie, asked.

"They awesome! They're so wise and beautiful but fun at the same time!"

"Where did they come from?" Aura asked.

"They travelled from the Indigo World, which as I understand it, is in another galaxy to the one that Earth resides in. They travelled with a part of their Golden City, and they are in that city in room 333 at the moment. We shall be introducing you to them, as soon as we have got you all settled in to the Academy."

"Should we show them their rooms now, Linen?"

"Yes, Aria, I think that would be best. I will post the notice of our next meeting on the board in your rooms."

The Angels and Faeries rose up, and followed Aria out of the main hall. Linen followed on, wishing that he could fly with them. He thought about asking Velvet again if he could have his wings back, but he hadn't had the chance. And somehow, the responsibility of running the School seemed easier to bear with a human body. If he was his usual tiny Faerie self, he felt that the burden may be too heavy.

*   *   *

"Hello, Cobalt."

Cobalt looked up at his Guardian Angel and nodded. "Hello, Angel."

"I know you are in turmoil, and I understand and feel your sorrow and fears, but I can assure you that all will be well. Keep the feelings of love and peace that you felt in Amethyst's presence in your heart and you shall find her."

Cobalt nodded, but he already missed his Flame. He could still feel the warmth of her hand in his. "Thank you, Angel. I wish I could have had longer with her though, it is the first time we have met, and I would have liked to have had more time to get to know her." He pictured Amethyst's face the moment he'd left her sat on the bench in the gardens. It had been so painful to let go.

"You already do know her. As only a Twin Flame could. But if you think you feel a depth of love for her here, just wait until you are human." The Angel smiled. "This period of separation will be worth it."

"I know you are right." Cobalt sighed then squared his shoulders and stood up straight. "What do I do now?"

"You must decide on your mission for this new life. Your general purpose for being on Earth is to bring about the Awakening. But often it is good to have a more specific mission on which to focus your energy."

"I will make it my mission to assist humans and Earth Angels in connecting to one another. I will also make it my mission to find Amethyst, because I truly believe that our connection will inspire others."

"Perfect choice, Cobalt. I look forward to assisting you. Please, call upon me whenever you feel the need. I am here for you."

Cobalt smiled. He would complete his missions, he felt sure of it.

"Peace, love and light be with you always."

"And with you." Cobalt closed his eyes, and pictured Amethyst's beautiful face one last time.

*　　*　　*

Linen was so tired he couldn't sleep. He and Aria had worked well past midnight to get everything set up ready for classes to begin the next day. He didn't know how he would possibly have coped without the mad green Faerie. When he would get stressed, she would lighten the mood instantly, making him smile with her innocence, her honesty and her clumsiness.

He shifted about, trying to get comfortable, knowing that he would need plenty of rest. The first day of classes was sure to have a few rough spots. If it all went smoothly it would be something of a miracle.

His mind wandered back to Aria, and he smiled into the darkness. Did she have feelings for him too? He'd thought about telling her how he felt, admitting that he liked her more than just as a colleague, but then he didn't want to make things awkward between them, and he certainly didn't want to push her away. It was probably best to keep his feelings to himself, at least for now.

He sighed and thought of Starlight. What did she think of it all? Was she happy with the way things were turning out? He got the feeling that she knew far more about it all than she had told him.

Linen turned on his side and started humming the song he had written for Aria quietly to himself. He thanked the Angels once more for her presence. She was more like an Angel than a Faerie to him.

*   *   *

Starlight couldn't stop smiling. It had been quite some time since she had felt so happy. She had seen all that had happened at the Academy, with Linen and Aria, and with the new staff, and it was all working out exactly as she had seen it. Despite her positive mood, her heart ached a little for Cobalt and Amethyst. She had watched Amethyst in the Leprechaun Garden, and could feel her pain. She wished she could comfort her fellow Angel, and tell her that she would find her Flame again, and they would be so happy together on Earth. But she refrained from meddling. There was a reason why souls had to go through the pain of loss, the pain of being separated from those that they loved deeply. It strengthened their will. Without that pain, they might never reach their true potential. Might never really figure out who they are. Which is why she had stayed out of Velvet's life too. She sighed, her good mood slipped and she felt a little melancholy.

She missed her sister. She missed their conversations. She missed Velvet's beautiful laugh, her wisdom, and her wry sense of humour. It had been lonely up among the stars on her own, ever since Velvet left so long ago, even though Starlight knew that her sense of the time without her was merely an illusion. In truth, Velvet was still with her, she just wasn't experiencing that layer of reality. She was the voice inside Starlight's head though. The voice encouraging her, pushing her forwards, keeping her going.

Starlight knew how it felt to be apart from her Twin Flame too. She knew the emptiness within her heart well. It had been so long since they had allowed themselves to have a life together, that she had all but forgotten the taste of his lips and the smell of his hair. They had a very business-like relationship now, and always kept as much distance as possible. Even though there was usually no one watching.

Starlight had hoped that perhaps her vision of the future of the Earth would show her and her Flame coming together again, but it seemed that their separation was to last eternity, as was decided so long ago. She did love to visit him though. And even though he had taken on the form of an old man, she could still see the young soul that she loved. The one with a sparkle in his smile, and a dimple in his cheek.

When they were together, his eye had never twitched.

Chapter Seventeen

The Indigo Child was excited when Linen and Aria came to get them for their first day of classes. "You have worked so quickly! Thank you, Faeries, we shall come at once."

She silently communicated with her siblings, who all left the Golden City and appeared at her side as Children. "Come, brothers and sisters, it is time to begin our journey." She nodded to Linen and Aria, and they nodded back.

"As you know the way, we shall wait here for you to return to wake the Crystals," Linen said.

"I will not be long."

The Indigo Child led the way to the main hall. The Children were all silent as they walked down the gleaming white corridors, looking around in awe.

Once they were in the main hall and seated, she returned to where Linen and Aria waited outside room 334 for her. They went in to where the Crystal Children stood motionless and silent. She approached the clear quartz point, and whispered in her ear.

"Awake, Crystal Child. It is time."

Within seconds, the clear crystal was transformed into the blonde Child, who was smiling radiantly at her. The Crystal Child smiled at Linen and Aria, thanked them, and then turned to awaken her kin with her beautiful voice.

The Indigo Child watched the large crystals of all colours

transform into Children, and she couldn't help but grin. It made her so happy to know that the Crystals would be with her and her siblings on Earth. It was going to be a tough mission, but she felt more certain of their success now. She wondered if Starlight had managed to contact any of the other Children in the galaxy. She hoped so.

They all went to the main hall, and the Crystals sat behind the Indigos, while the Indigo Child went to sit next to her sister. She looked up at the stage to see the new teachers hovering there nervously, waiting to be introduced by Linen who had taken his place centre-stage. The Indigo Child could see that the fear and doubt had melted away from the former fire Faerie, and that he was finally owning his power and his strength as a leader and as the one who was about to change the world. Knowing that someone like him was running the School and supporting the Indigos and the Crystals made her even more certain that they would succeed in their missions to Awaken the Earth.

"Now we have done the introductions, we are going to split you up into groups, and assign you a teacher who will be your guidance teacher. If you have any questions or problems at all, they will be your first port of call. To do this, we have decided to randomly assign you a number, which will appear on your left palm in a second," he looked at Aria and she grinned back and clicked her fingers.

The Indigo Child looked down at her left palm and the number 3 shone back at her in green glitter.

"Each of the teachers have a number above them," Linen continued. Aria clicked her fingers again and green glittery numbers appeared above the teachers. "They will come down from the stage and if you could form a group around the teacher who has your number, that would be great."

Considering the number of Children, there was little fuss or confusion, they all moved quickly to their teachers in an orderly way. The Indigo Child found her teacher, a male Faerie called Quercus, who seemed to be very calm and wise. The Indigo Child looked around and was pleased to see that they had deliberately mixed up the Indigos and the Crystals in the groups. It would create an interesting mixture of energy, and would also help them to learn how to understand each other, and therefore be able to relate to each other, when they reached Earth.

She tuned out the chatter around her for a few moments and wondered what it would be like on Earth, what it would be like to be human. Though they had been linked to some of their kin while they were on Earth for a short time, to experience it properly first-hand would be an entirely different thing. She just hoped that she was able to maintain contact with her siblings while on Earth. Not just with those with her on Earth, but also with those back home.

She smiled as she thought of her last conversation with the professor. He had contacted her through the Indigo link to inform her that he had arrived back in the Indigo World, and was eagerly exploring his old haunts. He had become something of a celebrity, as the Indigos had never known one of their kin to be gone for so long, even to be cut off, only to return. She knew that he would keep the place running smoothly while she was fulfilling her mission, but she couldn't help but wish, just a tiny bit, that she was back home too.

*   *   *

Leon heard through the whispers of his fellow trainees about the arrival of the Crystal Children. He had seen some Angels and Faeries flying about, and guessed that they must be the new teachers for the School. There was a weird energy in the air, as though the Academy was literally transforming and morphing into the new School, while the trainees continued about their day.

He received daily proof of his visions as he watched things

happening that he had already Seen in his mind. At times he got confused over what was real and what was a vision as he was Seeing so frequently now. It was a good thing that he spent so much time alone, he would have confused anyone who spent any time with him.

He did wonder if he should have made more of an effort to make friends though. Several of the trainees had now been called to Earth, including his roommate, Cerise. He lay back on the soft grass in the Angelic Garden and closed his eyes, remembering saying goodbye to her.

"I've been called, Leon." Cerise had smiled at him, but Leon had seen the hint of fear and hopelessness in her eyes. He knew that she had only waited to answer the call because she was hoping that Leon would be able to reassure her that all would be well. That she would make a difference, and that they would Awaken the world.

But he didn't know if any of that was going to happen. He had not Seen it. He also knew that it didn't matter. He stepped forwards to hug her, realising then that he enjoyed the embrace of another being. "You will be amazing. Just remember who you are. And remember that if you need help, all you need to do is ask the Angels."

He knew he was being vague, but he also knew that he couldn't lie to her. Old Souls could detect lies too easily.

She squeezed him gently. "Thank you, Faerie. I appreciate that." She pulled back and Leon could see in her eyes that she had hoped for more comfort, but that she also had a little more hope than before.

Just as she closed her eyes to answer the call, Leon smiled and whispered, "Say hello to Corduroy."

Leon remembered her eyes snapping open to look at him the second she disappeared, and wondered if he shouldn't have said it. But then perhaps it didn't matter. As soon as she was born on Earth, her slate would be wiped clean, just like everyone else's. He sighed and opened his eyes, and stared at the blue sky above, the white clouds swirling happily. He'd had no visions of the weather while he had been at the Academy. Unsurprising, considering the weather was controlled by the team who kept the gardens. It had been odd though. Visions of the weather had made up the majority of what he Saw in the Elemental Realm. He wondered if that would be the case when he was human.

When he thought about having a clean slate, he worried again whether that meant he would lose his ability to See. He really didn't think he could cope with being blind. With having to wait to see what was going to happen, like everyone else. He had come to rely on his precognition, perhaps a little too much.

His thoughts drifted to Velvet for no particular reason, and suddenly he saw her lying on a couch, her hair wet and her leg bleeding with the bone protruding through the skin. A feeling of nausea washed over him, making him gag, and the vision slipped away. He swallowed a few times, and shook his head, trying to shake the gruesome sight out of his mind.

When he felt calm again, Leon wondered if he should tell Velvet about the many visions he'd had of her. And of Laguz. Though he had not seen them together, he had seen himself with each of them. He found it difficult to believe that their common link might be him. Why him? He was not special in any way. He was just an ordinary Faerie.

But clearly, he had a very important part to play.

*   *   *

The first session with the Children had gone well, Linen felt, as he sat at his desk a few hours later. It was now early in the afternoon and the Children were all in their new groups, being looked after by their guidance teachers. Linen had decided to keep that part of the format from the Academy, as it made sense that the Children knew who their first port of call was if they had a problem. Though he felt that there would be very few problems, as the Children were so much more evolved. They had so far handled everything with a grace and ease that was most definitely not human. He wondered if they would be able to adapt to Earth as well as they had adapted to being at the School.

Linen sat back in his chair and a thought suddenly occurred to him. Perhaps they should have insisted that the Children stay in their human forms while at the School, and not go back to their original forms at night and in-between classes. After all, that was what the Earth Angel trainees at the Academy had to do, so they could get used to it. His shoulders slumped at the idea. He still ached to fly, to be a Faerie again, and it bothered him that Aria could still zip around while he felt so heavy. Could he really inflict that upon the Children too?

He decided to ask the Indigo Child and the Crystal Child what they thought. He knew that they would choose the right option for their brothers and sisters, and then he wouldn't have to make the decision by himself. After all, like he had said to the teachers, they were all there to work together. He would not be the one to make all the decisions, but to listen, to learn, and to lead them in the right direction.

Linen tidied up the paper work on his desk, then decided to use the few spare minutes he had to visit the Elemental Garden. It felt like an age since he had been there last, and he had made a promise to Aria to relax and do something silly every day.

He stood up, pictured his favourite toadstool in his mind, then closed his eyes and clicked his fingers. Before he opened them, he could hear giggles.

"Linen! What are you doing here?"

Linen opened his eyes to see Aria perched on the toadstool, with her group of Crystal and Indigo Children sat on the grass before her. He raised an eyebrow. "Is there something wrong with your classroom, Aria?"

Aria blushed a little, like a child being told off for being naughty. "No, it's okay, it's just well," she shrugged her tiny shoulders. "It's hard to teach about nature when you're indoors. I thought it would be much better, for the Children, of course, if we were outside in the gardens. I thought it would, um, help with their learning." She grinned at Linen, looking pleased with her own explanation and Linen's heart melted.

He didn't think it was in any way possible to be angry or annoyed with Aria. "Of course," he smiled at the Children, and a couple of them grinned back. "I think that makes perfect sense, good thinking."

Aria beamed at him, and he knew then, with a shadow of a doubt, that he was madly in love with her. Afraid that his feelings may be showing on his face, he decided to move on quickly.

"I won't interrupt your class any further, please do continue." He walked quickly down the cobbled path towards the Angelic Garden, but passed through there when he saw that it was full of trainees and second-years on a break. He didn't want anyone to see his flame-red cheeks and question why. He reached the archway to the Atlantis Garden, and paused for a moment before entering. He never normally spent much time there, and somehow it felt like he was entering a different world.

When he approached the bench in the centre of the garden, he was surprised to see a statue of Laguz standing in front of it. Unlike the rest of the golden statues, this one was made of gleaming marble. The eyes were as vibrant as Laguz's own, and it unnerved Linen slightly when he met them, as he had the feeling that perhaps Laguz was watching him. Shaking his head at his thoughts, Linen settled on the bench and considered the presence of the statue. He figured that Velvet must have created it to fill the gap that Laguz had left behind. The sunlight shone down on it, making it glisten. Linen wondered if Velvet would manage to find Laguz again, or if her fears were realised, and too much time would have passed by the time she got there. His heart felt heavy at the thought that they might not get to be together. Despite the fact that he had yet to confess his feelings or take action, Linen knew that he would feel incomplete without Aria. That he would feel lost if he could not see her smile and hear her giggles. He was glad that she seemed to have completely recovered from her upset that morning, when Amethyst had pushed her away and refused her help.

Aware that time was slipping away and that he needed to visit the new classes to check that the new staff were doing okay, he stood and although he felt a bit silly doing so, he bowed his head to Laguz's statue.

"I hope you are reunited with your Flame once again, Laguz. Good luck, brother."

He closed his eyes and pictured Herkimer, then clicked his fingers.

*   *   *

Starlight was so pleased when Amethyst was called. She knew that despite the tough journey ahead for the Angel, she was going to make such a huge difference. She would be one of the way-changers on the planet, bringing the Awareness of the other realms to the humans. She wished that she could bring Amethyst and her Flame together sooner than was planned, but she knew that she would have to leave things as they currently were meant to be.

Starlight knew this even more clearly now, because at the moment that Amethyst answered the call to Earth, Starlight's vision that had been flickering and changing had started to become more solid. Parts of it had become more vivid, and had fixed in place.

Starlight wanted to celebrate by sharing the news with the

ones she loved the most, but she knew that was the one thing she couldn't do. Instead, she shone more brightly, beaming down on Earth all her love and beauty, knowing that things would turn out well after all.

Chapter Eighteen

Linen felt drained when he finally fell into his bed that night. It had been an emotionally tiring day, and his heart had hurt watching Aria being so upset. Her very best friend, a former Angel called Amethyst, had been called to Earth. Amethyst was excited because her Twin Flame, Cobalt, had already left, and she had hoped to follow him quickly so that she could find him once again.

But Aria had been heartbroken. Amethyst was her closest friend at the Academy, and indeed, the closest friend she had ever had, besides Larry. Linen hoped that Aria would soon bounce back to her normal crazy self. She always lifted his spirits and energy when she was near him. They'd stayed up late, talking, and Linen had got the impression that Aria didn't want to return to her room alone, now that both her roommates had left for Earth. He was sure that there were some empty staff rooms, he would ask Velvet if Aria could move into one of them, so that she was closer to the office. Then she wouldn't have to sleep in a big room by herself with empty beds.

If Linen was being honest with himself, he would admit that really, he wanted Aria here with him, in his room. But he just couldn't bring himself to declare his feelings to her. He wasn't sure if it was the size issue, him being in a human body and her being such a tiny little Faerie, or if it was because he wanted to remain professional. He also feared that if she didn't feel the same way, it would affect their working relationship. The School was going so well, the last thing he wanted to do was cause problems and make things awkward.

It barely felt as though he had closed his eyes for a few minutes when he awoke the next morning. He all but fell out of bed, dressed in his yellow robes and made his way to the office.

"Good morning, Linen," Velvet called out as he entered.

He nodded in reply and his silence prompted her to look up from her desk. She raised an eyebrow.

"Everything going well?"

Linen nodded again, and sat heavily behind his desk. "Just a bit tired," he finally replied, his mouth opening wide in a yawn.

"You do know that we are not on Earth, don't you, Linen?"

Linen frowned. "Of course, why?"

"On Earth, you may have no choice over your tiredness. But here, you do." She smiled at him. "Energy and rejuvenating your spirit are merely a request or click away."

Linen sighed. "You're right." He shook his head. "I was so busy, and got so tired, that I forgot that I could do something about it."

"It happens to us all."

Linen closed his eyes. He visualised himself feeling refreshed and rejuvenated, having had a deep sleep and a lazy day in the sunshine. He breathed in deeply and clicked his fingers. When he breathed out and opened his eyes, he felt as though every fibre of his being had been renewed. He felt like his old fire Faerie self again. He smiled at Velvet who smiled back.

"I trust that all is going well with the School?" she asked.

"Yes, everything is moving along perfectly, actually. There's just a lot more to this job than I imagined."

Velvet chuckled. "Believe me, I know what you mean."

"There was something I was going to ask you. Now that

Aria's roommates have both left, I wondered if Aria could move into one of the staff rooms. I assume there must be some spare ones in the same wing as me, now that some of the professors have left."

Velvet nodded. "Absolutely. I cannot see a problem with that. It makes sense for her to be living closer to the office anyway."

"Great, I'll ask Aria later."

"Ask me what?"

Linen looked up to see Aria enter the office, a questioning frown on her face.

"Good morning, Aria." Velvet stood. "I hope you both have a good day, I must be getting to my first class." With a click, Velvet left, and Aria turned to Linen.

"Ask me what?" she repeated.

Linen smiled. "It was nothing major, I was just suggesting to Velvet that we ask if you want to switch rooms."

"Switch rooms? To where?" Aria settled in her chair.

"To one of the staff rooms in this wing. You'll be closer to the office then."

Aria smiled, but Linen could see that the trauma of the day before was still causing her pain. "It would be nice to be closer to here. I'll be sad to leave the room I shared with Amethyst and Tim, but maybe it's good to have a fresh start." She nodded. "Yes, I think it's a good idea."

"Great. I can help you move later if you like."

"No need. I don't have many things in the room. I'll do it after class at lunchtime."

"Maybe we could meet in the gardens this evening, if you're not busy. It feels like ages since we just sat and talked."

Aria's face lit up, this time with a smile that reached her green eyes. "I'd really like that. We have been too busy lately."

"That's settled then." Linen finished sorting through his paperwork and glanced at the time. "Have you got a class this morning?"

Aria shot up off the stool. "Oops! See you later." She zoomed out of the door before Linen could say goodbye.

He shook his head and smiled to himself. She really did brighten up his day.

Feeling full of energy, Linen decided to go for a walk around the gardens before his meeting with Citrine. She had some ideas for some new classes for the Children and wanted to run them by him.

*   *   *

As more trainees answered the call to Earth, Leon became glad that he had not made many friends. It seemed that his fellow trainees were going through many goodbyes, and saying goodbye was not Leon's favourite thing to do. Perhaps that was why he found it difficult to form relationships that involved more than the occasional conversation or hug.

One afternoon, in the middle of his Manifestation class with his guidance professor, Chiffon, Leon blinked as sunlight suddenly beamed down on him, almost blinding him. The classroom ceiling had disappeared and was replaced by a bright blue sky. His classmates and Chiffon also disappeared, and Leon looked around the empty white room, wondering what information this vision was supposed to hold.

Then, out of the blue sky, a clear, multi-faceted crystal appeared. It lowered down until it was at the perfect angle for the sunlight to refract through it and create rainbows on the white walls. It began to turn slowly and Leon gasped at the sight of the beautiful little rainbows dancing around the room.

"Are you okay, Leon?"

Leon blinked and the rainbows faded away, leaving him feeling a little deflated. He looked up into Chiffon's concerned face and nodded. "Yes, I'm fine, thank you."

Chiffon smiled, but didn't look too convinced. "Okay. You just seemed to be somewhere else just then. I thought that maybe you had heard the call."

Leon shook his head. "No, I was having a vision. They seem to be coming more and more frequently, I do apologise for interrupting class."

"A vision of what?" Chiffon returned to the front of the class, and waited for his answer.

"I'm not sure exactly," Leon lied, not wanting to share the details. "I usually write down or draw what I See, and sometimes I can make sense of it later."

"Very well," Chiffon turned to the class and continued her lesson. Leon knew that she wasn't fooled by his lie, but she seemed to respect his unspoken request for privacy. He couldn't concentrate on the rest of the lesson, but Chiffon didn't call on him again, so he got away with it. Once safely in the Elemental Garden after class, Leon took his worn notebook out and quickly sketched the vision, but couldn't quite capture the beauty of the rainbows with his simple pencil. He had no idea yet what the dancing rainbows represented, but he did know that seeing them had given him so much hope, he believed that they must be a positive sign.

*   *   *

Starlight watched the Rainbows arrive at the Academy, and saw the delight on Velvet's face when they had lit up the room. She wished she could have taken her sister to their world. She would have loved it. There just wasn't any room to be gloomy in their multi-coloured haven.

She closed her eyes and let the future of the world run through her mind like a high-speed, high-definition movie. When it got to the last part, more of it had become clear, and defined. Though the very end was still a little hazy. When the last image faded away, Starlight smiled and wiped the crystalline tear from her cheek.

It seemed that one day she would indeed be able to take

her sister to the Rainbow World. Because in the future, she would be coming home to her.

Starlight sighed. She couldn't wait for that day. Being the Angel of Destiny was a lonely job at times. But she knew that even if she went back to the moment she decided to take on the role, she wouldn't choose differently. She couldn't imagine an existence where she didn't look after the Universe and its inhabitants.

She wondered if it was time to share the good news with Gold, but decided that perhaps he wasn't meant to know. In truth, she was just looking for an excuse to go and visit him. But then, why did the Angel of Destiny need an excuse to do anything?

A smile on her face, Starlight closed her eyes and pictured her Flame.

*   *   *

Linen called an evening meeting with the teachers of the School, to discuss the arrival of the Rainbows. He looked around the room at the Faeries and Angels, and couldn't help but grin widely at them all.

"It seems that we are doing something right. The third stage of Children have arrived."

There were a few oohs and aahs, Aria bounced up and down excitedly next to him.

"They are beings of pure light, and so will not need teaching, or any assistance, but I urge you to go and visit them. They are very wise and seem to have all the answers." He looked at Aria and noticed that she was blushing. He wondered what she had heard when she had held the Rainbow earlier that morning. His head had been spinning all day, yet he also felt like he was floating on a cloud. The arrival of the Rainbows seemed to make the possibility of the Golden Age even more certain. After all, the Rainbows wouldn't have travelled all the way to the School if they didn't believe they would be going to Earth.

"So the Golden Age really is going to happen?" Jade asked, looking a little awed at the idea.

"It certainly looks like it."

"With the Rainbows on Earth the Golden Age has to happen!" Aria said, hovering above her seat in excitement.

"Will there be more Children coming?" Quercus asked.

Linen shook his head. "No, I think that's all of them now. So we will just focus on teaching the Indigos and Crystals everything we can, then when the time is right, the Rainbows will go to Earth too."

"Do you honestly think there are enough Children to make the changes needed on Earth?"

Linen smiled at Citrine. "Yes, I do."

"How can you be so certain?" the Angel asked.

"Because though there are only a hundred Indigos and two hundred Crystals, there are thousands of Rainbows. They are going to light up the world so brightly, the Golden Age will be inevitable."

*　　*　　*

"We have been called, Sister. We must go to Earth."

The Indigo Child looked up at her siblings, and unexpectedly, tears formed in her eyes. She didn't wipe them away, but let them fall to the ground.

"My brothers and sisters, I wish you all the love and happiness possible in your new lives on Earth. Please keep in touch, I think it should be possible to remain connected - even when you are human and we are still here."

Each of them nodded, their usually happy expressions sombre. "Will it be very dark there?" the smallest one asked.

The Indigo Child smiled and took his hands, being the smallest of them all, she was still smaller than he. She looked into his deep blue eyes. "You are going to shine so bright, that darkness will not survive in your presence."

His smile lit up his face, and she could see that the fear had melted from his eyes.

She held her arms out. And as one, the Children rushed into her embrace and for several moments they all hugged.

"I will not forget any of you," she whispered. "You will always be my family."

Then, before she could say another word, they whispered their goodbyes and answered the call. Her arms fell to her sides, suddenly empty. "Goddess," she whispered to the empty room. "Take good care of them, please."

Unable to stand the quiet stillness, the Indigo Child decided to visit the Rainbow Children. The hallways were empty as she walked along slowly. Her heart was aching and hollow. Though she knew she would see them again, saying goodbye to her fellow Indigos broke her heart a little every time. She reached the room and once safely inside, she turned into her natural form, so that she could interact with the Rainbows more easily.

"Greetings, Indigo Child," the Rainbows said. "What brings you here in despair?"

The Indigo Child wove in and out of the Rainbows, allowing their coloured lights to lighten her own blue light.

"Only a few of my brothers and sisters have left so far, but I miss them already. What if I have sent them to a hellish place where they will not be cared for?"

"They are still connected to you, you need only tune into their energies and you can communicate with them easily. They are not lost. And though Earth is a difficult place, and they may suffer hardships and pain, they will also experience joy and happiness. They are going to change the world."

The Indigo Child slowed up and hovered just underneath the clear, faceted crystal that the Rainbows emanated from. "But they do not understand pain, or hardship, or suffering.

They will not be able to cope."

"I think you underestimate them," came the soft reply. "They understand that the changes they seek to make will not come easily. They understand that they will be challenging structures that have been in place for a long time. They know they will meet resistance, and that they will be forced to conform. But through the strength of your connections with one another, and through your deep knowledge and wisdom and inner light, you and your family will prevail."

The Indigo Child's spirit lifted, and her feelings of melancholy were swept away from her. Her light shone more brightly, and her feelings of hope were renewed.

"Thank you, Rainbows," she said. "I knew this was the right place to come. You have helped me greatly."

"That is our purpose. Please visit us whenever you wish. Even if it is merely to enjoy our light."

"I will do that." The Indigo Child moved towards the door, and just before reaching it, she resumed her human form. She looked back at the dancing Rainbows in the sunlight and smiled. "See you soon," she whispered.

Outside, in the hallway, she paused to take a deep breath, anchoring the feeling that she'd just experienced deeply into her soul. Then she set off for her afternoon class. Just as she was about to enter the classroom, one of her brothers found her.

"I have been looking for you," he said.

"What is it, my brother?" she asked.

"I have been called to Earth, but I have not answered yet because I have information that I feel I should share with Velvet. Do you think it is wise for me to do so?"

The Indigo Child frowned. "If you have the intuition that you must tell her, then it is wise to do so. Do you feel she is meant to know?"

He nodded. "Yes, it feels as though we cannot possibly succeed on Earth if she does not understand these things."

"Then you must tell her." The Indigo Child stepped forwards to hug him. "I have already said goodbye to many of our kin today, I'm not sure I can handle too many more. So I will not say goodbye, but I will say Goddess bless you, may your life be beautiful."

He hugged her tightly. "I will contact you when I can."

The Indigo Child pulled back and nodded, not trusting herself to speak as she felt tears prickling her eyelids again.

He understood her silence and walked away, looking back once to wave to her.

She waved back then took another deep breath, composing herself before entering the classroom.

*   *   *

Despite his visions, it was still a surprise when Velvet asked Leon to stay after class that afternoon.

Once the other trainees had left, Velvet smiled at Leon. "Don't worry, there's nothing wrong, I just wondered if I could ask you a favour."

"Of course, Velvet. What is it?"

"I have come to realise that in the very distant past I was once a Seer. But I cannot See at the moment. I wondered if you would be able to help me See again."

Leon's eyebrows raised. A couple of his visions now suddenly made sense to him. "I would be happy to assist, Velvet. I will show you how I got started - perhaps it will help."

Velvet stood and nodded. "Thank you. Are you free this evening? I know it's short notice, and you probably have plans, but it's of great importance that I begin as soon as possible. We could meet in my office."

"This evening is just fine. I have no plans. Shall I be there at eight o'clock?"

"Eight would be perfect."

Leon nodded and headed for the door. "I'll see you then." He headed down the hallway towards the gardens, thinking that it would be a good idea to have some quiet time to meditate before his meeting with Velvet.

Was this how their connection was to begin? Was teaching her to See again going to lead to them meeting on Earth? He reached the Angelic Garden and settled onto the bench in front of the waterfall. The Academy was becoming noticeably quieter, as more trainees, second-years, and even Children, heard and answered the call to Earth. He had heard that the third stage of Children had arrived, and that they were Rainbows, which confirmed the vision he'd had. He wondered if he was supposed to go and visit them. Perhaps it would be a good idea. He wasn't sure if trainees were allowed to, but he was sure he could find them and visit for a short while.

His gaze blurred a little as he watched the water falling from the invisible cliff. The patterns and the light reflecting off the water was mesmerising, and within seconds, Leon found himself wrapped up in a vision. He looked around and recognised his surroundings from a previous vision. He appeared to be in the kitchen of a small cottage. He looked out the window and saw that it was dark. He moved towards the window and could just about see the waves rolling in on the sand, in the faint moonlight.

Leon moved into the next room, and saw Laguz sat on the sofa reading a book by the dim lamplight. Like he had noticed previously, Laguz's form was not solid, it rippled and moved. Leon wondered what that meant. Most people he saw in his visions looked real, but Laguz's appearance definitely had an illusory feel to it.

"I'm going to bed now." Leon found himself saying to Laguz. His voice sounded weird, but he couldn't pinpoint why.

Laguz looked up from his book and smiled, his form rippled with the movement. "Good night, hope you sleep well."

Leon nodded and moved to the door. "See you in the morning." He left the room and headed up the stairs. Just as he was about to open the door to his bedroom, he heard a voice.

"May I join you?"

Leon blinked and came back to the present moment. It took him a second to remember where he was. He looked towards the source of the voice and saw a beautiful young Child standing in front of the bench where he sat.

"Of course," he replied, moving up a little. The Child settled next to him and was silent for a while.

"Are you an Indigo Child?" he asked, not wanting to pry, but curious all the same.

The Child nodded and looked at him, taking in his whole appearance. "And you are a Faerie, though not a typical one. You are much quieter, more reserved. I like your energy."

Leon smiled. "Thank you. I must admit, I do keep to myself a lot. I find it easier."

The Child tilted her head to one side. "Easier? Why is that?"

Leon thought about it for a while. He wasn't sure whether or not to mention his Sight, but then he figured that the Indigo Child would understand it, as she seemed to See so much herself. "I am a Seer. And I frequently See snippets of the future. In the Elemental Realm, they were mostly weather-related, but here they have been varied and very frequent." Leon looked back towards the waterfall. "Because of this, I sometimes confuse my visions with reality, and so if I spent too much time with someone, I fear they would think I was mad." He had never admitted this worry to anyone before, but it felt liberating to do so. Even if it was a little scary too.

He felt a light pressure on his knee and looked down to see the Indigo Child's delicate hand patting it. "I think you underestimate your fellow souls. Especially those here. There are plenty who would understand your gifts. On Earth, it may well be a little tougher, but I hope you find people who want to get to know you." She sighed. "I too, have been underestimating my own kin. Thinking that they will be in situations they cannot handle. But do you know what? We need to have more faith. We need to believe in them more. I think they may well surprise us."

Leon smiled at the Child. "Thank you. You are right, of course. I think the other reason for not getting too close to anyone here was that I knew I would have to say goodbye to them all very soon, and that our time together would be short. And I wasn't sure I could handle that."

The Indigo Child smiled and shook her head. "That was exactly my problem too. Saying goodbye is something I find alien and very difficult, because on my planet, no one dies. There is never any need to say goodbye. When some Indigos left long ago to go to Earth, we lost connection with them and never heard from them again. After that, well, there was a hole left in me. I never shone as brightly as I used to before that. So coming here, knowing I would have to say goodbye to my kin, that I may never see them again..." her voice trailed off and Leon noticed her tears sparkling in the sunlight as they fell. He put his arm around her and she leaned into his side.

"I think we are most definitely in the same space, little Indigo."

"Dimensionally, mentally, spiritually and metaphysically," the Child agreed.

Leon chuckled. "Yes indeed. I am glad that you joined me today."

"Was I interrupting a vision? I remember now that you had a very serious look on your face, as though you were concentrating."

"I was having a vision, but there's no need to worry about it. I have them so frequently it would be impossible for people to interact with me without interrupting one."

"I do apologise, I would have waited had I realised."

"No need to apologise, really. I don't think the vision was

very significant. I have had several similar ones recently. They all just seem to be little pieces of a bigger picture that the Universe appears to want me to See."

The Indigo Child pulled back a little to look up at Leon. "May I ask what they are of? Are they of Earth?"

"Yes, they are. They are of the life on Earth that I am about to experience. Or at least, that is how I have been interpreting them."

"Are they good visions? Are you happy on Earth? What is it like there?"

Leon smiled at the Indigo Child's questions. "They are pleasant enough visions, I have Seen myself meet some Earth Angels who are here at the Academy." Again, he didn't mention that they were Velvet and Laguz. "I think I will be able to Awaken when I am there."

The Indigo Child smiled. "That is a good thing." She sighed. "I wish I could See my future. I want to know if I will find my kin again."

With those words, Leon found himself thrown into a vision. In quick succession, he saw a child being born and growing up, until she was about nine or ten years old. Though it was very quick, he could See that she had a positive effect on the humans that surrounded her, and she was also linked to many other Children; Indigos and as well as Crystals. The vision abruptly ended and faded into darkness. Leon didn't dwell too much on this, he wasn't sure he wanted to know what it meant. He blinked and refocused his eyes. He looked at the Child who was watching him silently.

"You will have a beautiful life. You will retain your powers as an Indigo Child and you will have a positive effect on all those that you come into contact with. You will also find many of your kin. You will find the Crystals, also." Leon smiled. "Your Earthly beauty cannot hold a candle to your true self, but you are beautiful all the same." Leon could see the fear and tension melt from the Child's face as she smiled back.

"Thank you, Faerie. You have no idea what it means to me to know that my human life will be a good one." She hopped off the bench. "I think I will go spend some more time with my brothers and sisters before they are called." She reached out and patted Leon's knee again. "I hope to see you again."

"I hope so too," Leon replied. He watched the small Child walk away down the path towards the Academy. When she was out of sight, he turned his gaze back to the waterfall. He figured it must be getting close to the time he would be meeting Velvet. He took a deep breath and stood up. He still felt a little nervous about his meeting with Velvet, but his time in the Angelic Garden and his conversation with the Indigo Child had given him a deep feeling of calm. He set off towards the Academy, planning to stop off at his room first. As he walked, his nervousness began to fall away, and was replaced with a feeling of anticipation, and hope.

Chapter Nineteen

"Do you think the Rainbows would agree to us taking groups of the Indigos and Crystals to see them? I think they could learn so much just by being among them, don't you think?"

Linen nodded. He loved it when Aria started coming up with new ideas. She would get so passionate about them that her eyes would sparkle and she would emanate a hyperactive energy that helped to distract Linen from his thoughts for a while. For the last few days it had been bothering him more and more that he had not told the beautiful soul in front him that he loved her. He lived for the moments spent in her company, and he was so very thankful that he had been asked to leave his human life behind and become the Head of the new School. At this point, Linen just couldn't imagine existing without her.

"Do you really think that the Rainbows will be able to stay so optimistic and light when they are on Earth?"

Linen blinked and tried to focus on Aria's words. "I hope so. I really don't see how we can move into the Golden Age unless they do. I think their presence is the key to it all working out."

Aria nodded. "I suppose I should go and prepare for my class tomorrow. I want to be ready for them. It seems like no matter how early I think I am, my Children are always lined up outside the door, waiting for me."

Linen smiled. "They must be eager to learn from you."

"I guess so." Aria frowned. "Though at times I wonder if I am teaching them enough. It seems like all I'm doing is telling them stories about the Elemental Realm and talking about plants and trees and growing things."

"All of which is important stuff. Hopefully they will connect with former Faeries on Earth, and together they will begin to teach the humans to respect and care for their planet. To encourage them to build homes that enhance, and not destroy the land, and to live in harmony with nature." Linen couldn't help himself, he reached out and put his hand on Aria's shoulder. He thought she blushed a little, but he couldn't tell, the red flush of her cheeks could have just been from her excitement.

"You're doing a great job, Aria." The feel of her skin beneath his hand was so distracting, he was finding it difficult to form coherent sentences. He pulled his hand away. "I should do some planning work too. More Indigos are being called, and I need to make sure that everything is going according to plan."

Aria smiled. "I'm sure it is. You are awesome." She flew towards the door. "See you in the morning."

"Good night, Aria," Linen replied. He watched the door reappear behind her and sighed. Watching her leave was getting more difficult with each passing day. He shook his head and silently instructed himself to concentrate on the matter at hand.

He was so engrossed in his paperwork that he didn't even notice Velvet click her fingers softly and leave the room.

*   *   *

"Starlight. Lovely to see you as always."

Starlight had to restrain herself from kissing his wrinkled cheek. "Hello, Gold."

Gold smiled. "And to what do I owe this unexpected pleasure?"

Starlight shook her head. "Must there be a reason for us to meet?" She reached out to touch his arm. "In all honesty I couldn't think of a reason to come, and then I realised that I didn't need an excuse."

Gold was quiet for a moment, looking down at her hand. He sighed before looking up into her eyes. "Do you find it as difficult as I do?" he whispered, taking Starlight by surprise. They never spoke of their love.

She nodded slightly, stepping towards him. "More difficult than you could possibly imagine, Gold."

Gold bit his lip, his eyes searching hers, his right eye still, for once. "Do you regret choosing this separation?"

Starlight sighed. "Yes. But I also know I wouldn't have chosen otherwise. And neither would you."

Gold closed his eyes, and it broke Starlight's heart to see a tear slide down his cheek. She reached up and wiped it away. "Don't cry, my love." She pressed her hand against his chest. "We are one," she whispered, "This separation is nothing but an illusion, for I am with you always."

Gold nodded, and his form shimmered and rippled, showing his younger-looking self underneath; the way he had looked when Starlight had first met him. She couldn't stop herself this time, nor did she want to. She leaned forwards and closed her eyes a second before her lips touched his. Without a moment of hesitation, Gold responded, pulling her close to him, kissing her urgently.

After a few moments, they both became aware of another soul at the same time. They abruptly pulled apart, and Starlight looked around to see a figure walking through the dense mist. She looked back at Gold and their eyes met for a moment. A million unsaid words and emotions flitted between them. She nodded in acknowledgment of them, then left.

Back home among the stars, Starlight allowed her own

tears to fall. And whispered the words she wished she had said.

"I love you, Gold."

*   *   *

Though they had not made firm arrangements to meet, Leon knew that the Indigo Child would be there when he arrived in the Angelic Garden. The sunlight glinted in her long golden hair, making her seem even more ethereal. He approached slowly, not wanting to frighten her. As he reached the bench, the Child turned and smiled at him.

"I was hoping you would be here," she said. "Would you like to join me?"

Leon nodded and sat next to her on the bench. They sat in easy silence, listening to the waterfall and the occasional chirp of a bird nearby.

"How are things with you?" the Child asked softly.

"They are good. Most of the trainees have left now. There is just one other left in my class with me. I don't imagine it will be very long before I am called too."

"Are you excited?"

Leon looked sideways at the Child. There was something about her that made him feel like he could be completely honest. He had never felt so at ease in another soul's company. "Yes, though I feel apprehensive too. I feel like my role in the Awakening on Earth may be bigger than I had previously imagined."

The Indigo Child smiled. "Every single Earth Angel and Child of the Golden Age is an important part of the Awakening, Faerie. What do you imagine your role to be?"

Leon blushed. "I didn't mean to sound egotistical, or that I was above anyone else, that wasn't-"

"I know." The Indigo Child patted his arm. "I did not mean to accuse you of being above anyone. I was just interested to know what you felt was a bigger role in the Awakening."

Leon sighed. "I have seen myself on Earth, with Velvet and Laguz. And I feel that their reunion, their energy and their love will be instrumental to the fate of the world. And somehow, I will be a part of it. It has already begun, I have been trying to assist Velvet in regaining her ability to See."

The Indigo Child nodded. "I now understand what you meant. I believe that their part will be very important too. Though I fear that because of that importance, if they fail to reunite, then the world will fail too." The Indigo Child was silent then, gazing at the falling water.

"You See more than you let on, Indigo, what have you Seen? Do you think they will fail?"

"From what I know of humans, I believe that it is possible for it to go either way. It is not something that I feel able to predict."

"Me either," Leon agreed. "Though I have Seen myself with both of them, I have yet to See them together in my visions."

The Indigo Child smiled up at him. "I believe that you will do your best to assist them." She tilted her head to one side. "Would you like to go and visit the Rainbow Children?"

Leon's heart lifted at her words. "I would love to. I had hoped to meet them before I left."

The Indigo Child hopped off the bench and held her hand out to him. He stood up and took her hand, and she led him to where the Rainbows danced in the sun.

*　　　*　　　*

For several hours after their meeting in the Leprechaun Garden, Linen sat in his room, reliving their conversation. He remembered the look in Aria's eyes, and what seemed to be left unsaid between them. Now that all of the second-years were gone, nearly all of the trainees had left, and the Children were already leaving, Linen had more time to ponder what was to happen next. When he asked Aria what she would like to do, she didn't seem to know how to answer his question. He wondered what she was really thinking when she said she didn't know. He wondered if she was waiting to know his preference. Could she really want to be where he was? His heart leapt at the thought, and once more, for the millionth time, he kicked himself for letting another day pass without admitting his true feelings to her.

As ditsy as she appeared at times, Linen knew that she wasn't stupid, that she must have sensed how he felt, even if it was only a fraction of his true feelings. He just wished he was able to pick up on how she felt too.

His thoughts drifted to Velvet, and her desperate attempts to be able to See again. Though it was only a few weeks ago that he felt huge anxiety at the thought of losing her and her guidance, Linen now felt ready to run the School. He knew that he would be able to handle it. He also hoped that Velvet would leave soon so that she had a chance to be with Laguz. He knew he would be going crazy if Aria were on Earth and he was stuck in the Fifth Dimension. Just being in the room next to her rather than in the same room was difficult for him at times.

Starlight popped into his thoughts, and he smiled. He wondered if the Angel of the stars had been watching him. If she had seen all that he had managed to accomplish and if she had known all along what was going to transpire. He wondered if he would ever see her again. He got into bed and settled back onto his pillows and tried to close his eyes. Though there was less to do, he still had to be alert and able to lead the Children.

Just before he drifted into unconsciousness, he wondered if Starlight was proud of the Faerie boy who was helping to change the world. He knew that his mother on Earth would have been proud if she had known.

*   *   *

Starlight heard Linen's thoughts, and because she was feeling particularly sentimental in that moment, she closed her eyes and left her home, reappearing moments later on Earth, outside Linen's home. Or Mikey's home, rather.

In another blink of her eyes, she was inside, looking down at Mikey's mother. She had aged a lot in the last twenty-five years since Mikey had died. Starlight looked at the empty side of the bed and an unexpected tear came to her eye. She wondered if she had aged even more since Mikey's father had passed away.

She sighed. Perhaps she should have made Linen aware of his father's passing, so that he could have spoken to him before he moved onto the next stage of his evolution. But she hadn't wanted to distract Linen from his tasks. Since that dream meeting she had facilitated between him and his parents, he had seemed to be content. And after Aria had arrived in his life, he had given even less thought to the family he'd left behind.

Starlight looked down at Mikey's mother's lined face, peaceful and deep in sleep, and she decided to give her a gift. She closed her eyes and entered the sleeping woman's aura. She found the dreamspace dimension and connected with her soul. Then she let images of Linen run through her mind, of him running the School on the Other Side, of him bringing together Angels and Faeries, and of him doing his best to bring the world into an Awakening. She made sure that the importance of his role came through loud and clear, so that it was obvious why he'd had to leave Earth.

Though it lasted only a few moments, Starlight knew that those little film-like reels would be playing in Mikey's mother's mind throughout the night. She left the dreamspace and opened her eyes. Mikey's mother's eyelids were flickering, and her lips had curved up slightly, into a contented smile.

Starlight left, knowing that she would not visit her again,

but that she would see her one day soon, when she came home to the stars.

*   *   *

Leon and Amber left class at the same time, and found themselves heading in the same direction.

"Are you going to the gardens?" Amber asked.

"Yes, I usually spend my free time in the Angelic Garden."

"Not the Elemental Garden?"

Leon shook his head. "Before we got our human bodies, I spent most of my time there, but now I find it difficult to be in my old habitat."

"I can understand that. I like to sit in the Planetary Garden. I find it incredibly peaceful."

"I haven't really been there before."

Just before they entered the Angelic Garden, Amber smiled at Leon. "You should give it a try sometime, before you are called. If you relax enough there, gravity disappears and you float. It reminds me of when I had wings, which is probably why I enjoy going there."

"I miss having wings sometimes, too. I may well visit before I leave. I hope you don't think it rude, but my friend is just over there, and-"

Amber held up a hand. "Not at all. Please, go join her. I am going to another galaxy for a while." She winked at Leon and set off towards the Planetary Garden. Leon watched the former Angel walk away for a few moments then he turned towards the bench where the Indigo Child was sitting. Considering he had been a solitary Faerie for so long, it surprised him how much he looked forward to the company of the very wise and knowing Indigo Child every day. He found they had a connection, an understanding. And he very much hoped that they met again on Earth. He reached the bench and without a word, he sat next to her. He noticed immediately that she had tears gathering in her eyes, waiting to fall like crystals from her long lashes.

It felt inappropriate to say anything, so he just put his arm around her, and she leaned into his side. He wasn't sure if it was his ability to See or if it was just purely a deep empathy, but he felt the pain that she was experiencing from saying goodbye to yet more of her siblings. He sighed and wished that there was something he could say to soothe her. But he also knew that letting go and learning how to say goodbye was an important lesson that this otherworldly Child needed to learn.

The best he could hope to do was to ease her pain with his company.

"I know," he said softly. "It's all going to be okay."

He felt her shoulders shudder and she buried her face in his clothing. He held her tighter, hoping to comfort the one friend he had made here in the Fifth Dimension.

*   *   *

When he first heard it, he felt both elated and scared at the same time. After what felt like centuries at the Academy, thanks to his many visions, Leon was being called to Earth. He sat up in his bed and looked around at the empty room, feeling very lonely. He had a meeting scheduled with Velvet in the afternoon, so he would have to wait until then to answer the call. She hadn't Seen anything so far, and Leon knew that he wouldn't be able to leave until she had.

At least, that was what the Rainbows had told him. He smiled at the memory of the dancing beams of light, and of the tickly feeling of holding one in his palm. He had been impressed by the depth of knowledge the Indigo Child had, but the Rainbows had blown him away.

Their words had settled any remaining fears he had about his role in the Awakening, and what it would be like to live on

Earth. The flicker of fear he had felt when he heard the call had dissipated. Now he just felt a little sad at the thought of saying goodbye to his friend.

Though it was early, Leon got up, and dressed in his usual clothes. He looked around the room, his walls were still white and undecorated. He took his notebook from the bedside table and tucked it into his pocket. He looked around at the underwater themed decor and the quotes on Cerise's walls. He knew it would be the last time he saw this room, as he had no intention of returning.

He left the room, and set off for the gardens. They were completely empty in the early morning, ever-present sunshine. He slowly walked through each garden, pausing in the Planetary Garden to relax, to see if he could float in the way Amber had described. He was just about to sink into a deep mediation, while sitting cross-legged on a planet, when he heard the call for the third time. The voice was a little louder, and a little more insistent. He decided to move on from the Planetary Garden, in the hope that the Indigo Child may have foreseen his leaving and was waiting for him in the Angelic Garden. His heart sank when he saw the empty golden bench. But he went over to it and sat anyway.

He had been watching the waterfall for barely a few moments when he sensed her approach.

"You have sad news for me, Faerie."

It wasn't a question, but a statement. Leon turned to look at her where she stood next to the bench. He nodded. "I have been called, Indigo. It is time for me to go to Earth."

The Child nodded. A single tear fell but she smiled. "Though I still am not comfortable with the feeling of loss, I am getting used to saying goodbye."

Leon smiled back, and felt tears welling up in his own eyes. He held his arms open and the Child stepped into them. "The thing with saying goodbye, is that no matter how many times you say it, it still always hurts as much as it did the first time," he said, his own voice choked with tears. He felt her nod.

After a few moments, he pulled back slightly and looked into her beautiful, sad, wise face. "There is something I wish for you to have." He pulled his notebook out, and handed it to her. She took it, and looked down at the cover with a frown on her face.

"What is it?"

"Open it."

She opened the notebook to the first page, and smiled at the drawing she saw there. A few pages in, she gasped. "This is my city, my home!"

Leon smiled. "I thought it might be."

"How did you know what it looked like? It is not the part of the city that we brought with us here. It is what was left behind on our planet."

"I Saw it in a vision. Before you arrived at the Academy. Sometimes I write down my visions, but sometimes I See things that cannot easily be described with words, so I draw them."

The Indigo Child nodded and continued to turn the pages, reading the odd sentence every now and then. She paused and looked up at him. "Are you sure you want me to have this?"

"Yes. I know that I can entrust it to you. And I also know that the contents will not alarm you, because I am sure you have Seen more than I."

"I will take good care of it, Faerie." She sighed. "So you will be leaving today?"

Leon nodded. "I have a meeting with Velvet this afternoon, by which time I am sure that the call will be getting even more insistent. I will leave immediately afterwards."

"Okay." The Indigo Child closed the notebook and hugged it to her chest. "Thank you. For this, for our conversations. For your friendship."

Leon swallowed the lump in his throat and felt the tears

welling up again. He wasn't keen on displaying his emotions in public, but the sadness he felt right now was so strong, he couldn't help expressing it. "Thank you for your wisdom and beauty. And for taking me to meet the Rainbows. I have no fear of what awaits me on Earth now. I know that everything will work out exactly as it should."

"Yes it will." She took a deep breath and stood up from the bench. "Would you mind if I leave, and not say goodbye, so that I can imagine that I will see you here again?"

A tear slid down Leon's face as he nodded. "Yes." He reached out and took her hand, squeezing it gently. "I will see you again, Indigo."

The Child nodded. "See you soon," she said softly. She let go of his hand and walked down the path, back towards the Academy. Leon watched her go with a heavy heart. He let another tear fall before wiping his face with his sleeve. There was nowhere else he would rather be, so he decided to stay in the Angelic Garden, listening to the water falling and the call of the Angels, until his meeting with Velvet.

Then he would begin his next adventure.

Chapter Twenty

"Adrian?"

He heard her voice as though it was coming through fog, and he tried to grasp it, so that he didn't slip away into nothingness again.

"I'm here, I won't leave you, I promise."

He tried to nod, but his head felt too heavy. Mustering all the strength he had, he managed to open one eye, and he saw his twin sister sat next to his bed. His lips formed her name, but no sound came out.

"Don't try to speak, I know, little brother. I know." Though she had been born just three minutes before him, she had always called him her little brother. When they were younger, it would bother him, but now he knew that she had done it because she wanted to protect him. Because she cared so much for him. His heart hurt at the thought of leaving her, but the call to go home was so strong. There was something he needed to do, and he felt that if he stayed on Earth in his decaying body for much longer, he would miss his chance.

"I love you so much, Adrian. I know we don't say it very often, but I do."

Adrian closed his eyes and nodded his head a tiny fraction, hoping she would see his agreement. A voice called for him then, an Angelic voice so melodic, and so familiar.

Suddenly, feeling a surge of strength, he opened both eyes

and looked at Maggie. She seemed surprised by his sudden movement. His heart filled with love as he looked at his sister. "I love you, Maggie," he whispered. "But I need to go. They are waiting for me."

Her eyes widened and her grip on his hand tightened. Swallowing hard, she nodded. "I understand." Tears ran freely down her cheeks. "Is it okay if I stay here with you until you leave?"

Adrian smiled. "I would like that." His energy drained, he closed his eyes, and the last thing he heard before he slipped into the familiar darkness was Maggie's soft voice.

"Say hello from me."

*   *   *

Linen hadn't felt so free in a long time. His ecstasy at having his wings back was dampened only slightly by the fact that Velvet had left not long before. She had heard the call in the morning, and after speaking briefly with the Children, she had left.

"Hey, have you become a ditsy Faerie now that you have your wings back?"

Linen refocused his eyes and snapped out of his thoughts. He smiled at Aria. "No, I was just thinking about how amazing it felt to be able to fly again."

"What, even though I beat you both to the main hall and back again?" Aria teased.

Linen laughed. "Yes. I hadn't realised just how heavy that body was becoming." He flew around the office a few times. "I really hope I never have to lose my wings again."

Aria glanced over her shoulder at her own dragonfly wings. "I hope I never have to lose mine. Flying means so much to me."

Linen settled behind his desk. "I suppose we should get a little work done."

Aria nodded and took out her paperwork for her classes.

Linen tried to focus on his own work, but his mind kept intruding. The feeling of freedom wasn't just about the flying. He was now the same size as Aria. The same species. There were no reasons or excuses why they couldn't be together now. But yet the words still stuck in his throat. Why couldn't he just admit how he felt?

After a few minutes of internal wrestling, he looked up and noticed that Aria was crying.

"Aria, are you okay?"

*　　*　　*

"Greetings, Laguz."

"Angel!" Laguz threw his arms around the celestial being and hugged her tight, making her chuckle. "It's so good to see you."

"It is a pleasure to see you again. We have been calling you back for a while."

Laguz frowned and suddenly everything came back to him. "Velvet! Is she still here? You said last time I saw you that she would be."

His Guardian Angel nodded. "She is still at the Academy." She stepped to one side and gestured into the mist. "I am sure that you know the way by now."

Laguz smiled at the Angel. "Thank you." As he passed her, he reached out and touched her shoulder. She smiled at him and nodded.

He stepped into the thick mist and closed his eyes. He saw the Earth Angel Training Academy in his mind, and when he opened his eyes, the mists had cleared and it stood before him. It didn't look exactly as he remembered; the logo of the Angel and the world had been changed to a golden Earth surrounded by a circle of Children holding hands. Laguz smiled. The Children must have arrived at the Academy, which was a very good sign. He entered the foyer and quickly made his way to Velvet's office.

After yet another lifetime spent without Velvet by his side, he couldn't wait to take her back into his arms and hold her close. To breathe in the scent of her hair, to hear her laugh. His chest ached as he walked faster. He imagined the look on her face when she saw him again.

He skidded to a stop outside the office door, and in his hurry to enter, didn't even notice that Velvet's name was no longer featured on the golden plaque.

He stepped into the office and smiled at the sight that greeted him. After a few moments, he cleared his throat, his impatience getting the better of him.

The entangled Faeries flew apart from each other and stared at him in open-mouthed shock.

"Laguz! What are you doing here?"

*   *   *

"You called, Gold?" Though she knew from his worried expression that he had called her there for business reasons, her heart still beat faster in anticipation when she had heard his voice calling for her.

"Yes, we have a situation, and I just needed to check with you that it is all proceeding correctly." Gold sighed, looking even older and wearier than ever.

"What is it?"

"Laguz has returned to the Other Side and he went to the School only to find that Velvet left just minutes before. He wishes to return to Earth immediately, so that there is a chance for him to find Velvet."

Starlight nodded. "Yes, that's right. It was always going to happen this way, Gold. It is all unfolding as it should. You can inform the Angels that he is to be called back to Earth as soon as possible."

Gold frowned. "You always knew that they would miss each other? That Velvet wouldn't know he was coming for her?"

Starlight nodded. "You must think me cruel, to not have given her the information; so that she could have gone to Earth with a hopeful heart, rather than a heavy, sorrowful one. But I promise you, Gold, there is a reason for my silence. There is a reason for it all." She sighed. "It hurts me to cause her pain, you know how much I love her. But it is necessary, it's all for the highest good of everyone on the planet." She smiled at Gold and reached out to touch his arm. "For everyone in the Universe, for that matter."

Gold nodded, but the worried frown remained, and his eye began to twitch.

"What is it, Gold?"

Gold sighed. "You always could read me like a book." He shook his head. "It's just that they're not going to meet, are they?"

"They will meet. But they will not fully realise who the other is until it's too late."

"Couldn't I tell Laguz that? So that perhaps he has a better chance of realising it?"

Starlight shook her head, but she was smiling. "I had forgotten what a romantic soul you are. I showed you what is meant to happen. What will happen, if we grant them the right of free will."

"I know you are right. I will inform the Angels that he is to be called. Thank you, Starlight." Their eyes met and for a moment, the twitching stopped.

"I will see you again soon, Gold. You know you can call upon me at any time." He nodded and she closed her eyes and returned home. Though she felt a little sad, she knew that once Laguz was on Earth, the real work would begin. She let the future of Earth run through her mind again like a movie, and when it got to the end of the reel, it no longer flickered and faded, it was solid, the colours were bright and the futures of those involved were completely set.

She smiled.

*   *   *

"Angel! Thank you so much for calling me back to Earth." Laguz engulfed his Guardian Angel in another hug, and this time she did not laugh.

"I'm glad that you are pleased, Laguz, but are you sure you wish to return so soon? Most souls need time to rest and renew their energy and their spirit. Going back this quickly could be detrimental to you."

Laguz could not be swayed. "Velvet is on Earth. I need to be there. I need to find her and we need to be together. I'm sorry, Angel, if you feel that it is too soon, but I cannot wait another moment."

His Guardian Angel nodded. "It will not be an easy road, but I am here, available at all times, just call for me whenever you need my help."

Laguz smiled. "I will, I promise." He couldn't help but pull her into another hug. "I will try not to let you down."

"It's not even possible for you to do that. You are a beautiful, perfect soul, and I will love you unconditionally forever."

Laguz squeezed her tightly for a moment, then stepped back. He wiped away the unexpected tear that was running down his cheek.

"I love you too, Angel. Goodbye." He turned away from her and walked into the mist, determined to go to Earth and find his Flame.

As he disappeared, his Angel sighed. "See you soon, Laguz."

The Earth Angel Series:

The Earth Angel Training Academy (book 1)

Velvet is an Old Soul, and the Head of the Earth Angel Training Academy on the Other Side. Her mission is to train and send Angels, Faeries, Merpeople and Starpeople to Earth to Awaken the humans.

The dramatic shift in consciousness on Earth means that the Golden Age is now a possibility. But it will only happen if the Twin Flames are reunited, and the Indigo, Crystal and Rainbow Children come to Earth, to spread their love, light and wisdom.

While dealing with all the many changes, Velvet struggles to see the bigger picture. When she is reunited with her Flame for the first time in many lifetimes, her determination and resolve to fulfil her mission falter...

The Earth Angel Awakening (book 2)

'No matter how overcast the sky, the stars continue to shine. We just have to be patient enough to wait for clouds to lift.'

Twenty-five years after leaving the Earth Angel Training Academy to be born on Earth as a human, Velvet (now known on Earth as Violet) is beginning to Awaken. But when she repeatedly ignores her dreams and intuition, she misses the opportunity to be with her Twin Flame, Laguz. Without the long-awaited reunion with her Twin Flame, can Violet possibly Awaken fully, and help to bring the world into the elusive Golden Age?

Other books by Michelle Gordon:

The Doorway to PAM

Natalie is an ordinary girl who has lost her way. There is nothing particularly special about her or her life. She has no exceptional abilities. She hasn't achieved anything miraculous. Her life has very little meaning to it.

Evelyn is the caretaker at Pam's. The alternate dimension where souls at their lowest point find the answers they need to turn their lives around. The dimension dreamers visit, to help people while they sleep.

One ordinary girl, one extraordinary woman.

One fated meeting that will change lives.

The Elphite

Ellie's life is just one long, bad case of déjà vu. She has lived her life before - a hundred times before - and she remembers each and every lifetime.

Each time, she has changed things, but has never managed to change the ending.

This time, in this life, she hopes that it will be different. So she makes the biggest change of all - she tries to avoid meeting him.

Her soulmate. The love of her life.

Because maybe if they don't meet, she can finally change her destiny.
But fate has other ideas...

About the Author

Michelle lives in England, in the middle of the woods. When not writing and publishing her own books, she helps other Indie Authors with their own publishing adventures. She has known all her life that she was a writer. It is more of a calling than simply a passion, and despite her attempts to live in the normal world, she has finally realised that she would much rather live in a world of Angels, Faeries, Mermaids and Leprechauns.

Please feel free to write a review of this book on Amazon, or even just click the Like button. Michelle loves to get direct feedback, so if you would like to contact her, please e-mail **theamethystangel@hotmail.co.uk** or keep up-to-date by following her blog – **eata.wordpress.com.** You can also follow her on Twitter **@themiraclemuse** or 'like' her page on Facebook.

To sign up to her mailing list, visit:
www.michellegordon.co.uk

DARKHORIZONSMEDIA

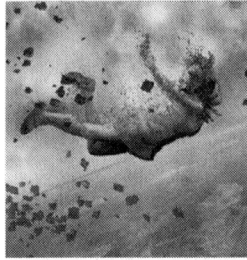

My name is Jason, and I am a Graphic Art Designer and Fine Art Photographer. I create art covers and do promotional photo-shoots for bands all around the globe, and create cover art for print and eBooks. Always ready to take on bigger challenges and adventures, I have recently become an On-set Stills Photographer and Graphic Design Artist for a feature film.

Over the years I have developed my own unique style, and every day I am driven by my passion to express myself through my art. I work closely with my clients to create the look and feel that they want, to best represent their own passions.

You can see my Fine Art Photography online:
facebook.com/mordecaiphotography

You can see my band cover art and graphic art on my website:
darkhorizonsmedia.com

If you would like to get in touch, please e-mail me on:
darkhorizonsmedia@gmail.com

designs from a
different planet

madappledesigns
.co.uk

In gratitude for the nourishing vibrational
energy of the trees that have sustained me for
so many years, I have created:

Sacred Tree Spirit

In this dream-like space, you can
receive intergrated therapies, emotional
and core-belief re-programming and
vibrational healing.
You can relax in the mineral spa,
watch life-affirming films in our
imaginarium, attend courses and shop
for handmade gifts.
Or you could just come along for a
drink and a cake to meet like-minded
people.

sacred-tree-spirit.com

Peace of Stone

9 Swan Court, Monmouth, NP25 3NY

Crystals

Jewellery

Gifts & Homeware

Crystal Therapy Treatments

Reiki Treatments

Hopi Ear Candling

Intuitive Workshops

www.peaceofstone.com

This book was brought to publication by
The Amethyst Angel.

These books were too:

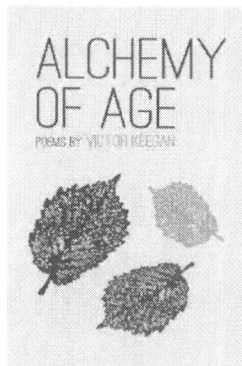

The
Amethyst
Angel

If you are an Author wishing to publish
independently and you are in need of
advice, or help with editing, formatting or
publishing, please visit us at
theamethystangel.com

62617422R00128

Made in the USA
Charleston, SC
19 October 2016